ONE TEAR
FOR GOD TRILLIONS
FOR
AMERICA

BY

GILBERT "GIL" ALVAREZ

ISBN: 978-1-4107-1554-8 (sc)
ISBN: 978-1-4107-1555-5 (e)

This book is printed on acid free paper.

Print information available on the last page.

1stBooks – rev. 03/12/2020

INTRODUCTION BY GILBERT "GIL" ALVAREZ

A love affair of a white thirdish female blond who is all American high class educated and former Miss America. Who falls in love with the "Egyptian," Omar Bin Mohammad the accused terrorist. The location is Palm Springs California. Palm Springs is no longer the traditional resort village little town from the 1900's. It has become a haven and political center for homosexuals and liberal radicals. Sarah the young blond lives in a shadow goverment below the Palm Springs foot mountains with her Jewish father. This fasinating story of fiction or non fiction? Make up our minds. We all have a bit of it in us. We all need a place for tears. But only in America can the real sobbing be heard of two liberal love birds. And a father and surgeon who not love their lifes unto their deaths. To save their loved ones and the world from its final distruction.

This book and story is about a would be terrorist. That was born in the country of Egypt of a humble family of ten kids. His name is Omar Bin Mohammad. Who calls himself Sabastian Mijarez of Mexican orgin to hide his real identity. Is An Islamic fundamentalist who denounces terror as a way to achieve Peace on earth. The morning of September 11,2001. He was part of Osama's Bin Laden Al-Qaida terrorist group to blow up the twin tower world trade center with The United States own commercial airplanes.

The morning of 911. He being on board on an airflight comming out of the state of Texas. Broke the oath he had taken with the Al-Qaida and never went through the terror plan to ambush the pilots and crash the plane into the world trade centers. Instead he went with the plane scheduled to its finale distination. Which was Los Angeles. California.

On the airplane he meets the very beautiful former Miss America Sarah Cunningham who owns a cosmetic company and is on her way to her home factory place in Los Angeles California. Miss Cunningham is a thirtish graduate of Standford the new Harvard university of the west. Sarahs Biological father is a former ambassador to Israel were he impregnated a young Palestinian out of wedlock who gave birth to Sarah Cunningham While Mr. William "Bill" Cunningham was married to his American wife of many years. Mr. Cunningham is the fall guy who saves his family from the worlds total destruction.

Sarah and Omar fall in love and take on the world to defend their freedoms. But their freedom has a price. In the twilight zone.

TABLE OF CONTENTS

"May love guide us all."
(Gil Alvarez)

CHAPTER 1

SEPTEMBER 11,2001

It was an early morning in southern Califronia when a 747 airliner was headed towards Los Angeles. The skys where passive blue. And two unknowns where traveling first class. A beautiful five foot seven inch blond. Who any traditional American family would love for her daughter.

Across the way was a handsome dark middle eastern looking man about twenty-one years of age. His eyes were glittering with passion and a hidden far away look. Very well dressed and manners was he. Dressed with a dark christ like beard. They bothed glanced at each other as if they wanted to reach out and touch.

Sarah was coming home from selling products that had to do with health and hygeine. She had been Miss Universe at the young age of twenty one. Now nine years later. She owned her very own cosmetic products. You wanted to make your face and body younger and healthier. She was the owner lock, stock and financial. Just give her a call. And she could supply you with it all. Her base company was in Los Angeles. Had fifty professionals working for her. Life was sweet but sour as she was plagued with out the love of her life. She had gone through two divorces in just ten years. Sarah the daughter of a well to do ambassador. During the Roberts administration. Could hardly realize that the world she grew up in. Was at odds with her new image. A millionares. And all the comforts any young thirty year old could want. She was way ahead also intellectually. Having been graduated in her class, tops from Stanford university in Humanism studies as a major and modeling as a minor.

She had worked over seas as a nurse assistant with Green peace organization.

Gilbert "Gil" Alvarez

Sabastian as he called himself. Is a very lonely withdrawn young adult. Age, Twenty-one years young. That says he is from Juanajuato Mexico. His soft mild voice makes him seem even younger. He could be any mothers dream son in middle class America. Once as a younger boy he says he hitch hiked from his state in Mexico to the tip of the country of Argentina. There he said he met the love of his life. A young seventeen year old basque girl who loved the rock group smashing pumkins and green day. But If not for the girls father. Sabastian would have married her. Now a few years later he finds himself all alone. His mother died in a car crash in Tijuana baja California Mexico. A northern coast town in Mexico in the tip of Southern California that borders the beautiful town of San Diego California. The ex- naval resort that onced defended the most powerful country in the world. Sabastians father he says lives at home. And has since remarried. The only thing to do now he believes is to go out on his own and find the job he loved best. Car racing. As a child he would watch on t.v. The great drivers like Mario Andretti, Parnely Jones and their sons. And when the professional car drivers came into his town. He would skep work and hurry down to the drag strip to watch them.

BOOM!! The radio in the 747 went. The passengers on board flight 234 were being adressed bout an explosion on the world trade center, twin tower buildings. They had just been crashed into what is believed by two large airplanes. No one knows now what has happen. Maybe an accident. As for now Sarahs and Sabastian's 747 was going in for a landing in the Los Angeles international airport.

The airline stuardess cautious everyone to fasten their seat belts. There is a wind turbulance on the horizon. The 747 is being piloted by two of Americas very best two young airforce officers, recent graduates from Colorado Springs airforce academy. There are also American fighter jets crusing the skys and patroling the area.

We are now comming in for the landing ladys and gentelmen. The stuardess cautioned. Please stay calm. When we land please do not stand up or unfasten your seat belts. We will give the okay when to get up. We could run into some difficulties on the ground. If you have any relatives or loved ones waiting. They have been cautioned to wait for you at the waiting areas. And again thank you for cooperating and flying the airwaves. Have a safe home trip.

As the 747 is being guided to land. We see police and military guards and units unbarking on the airport run lines and station gates. Sabastian seems at odds and nervous as Sarah turns over to eye him. Sabastian has a tear on his eye and bends his head down. Sarah noticing stares as if knowing something was wrong. She whispers in a loud tone. Is everything alright? Hello? hello?

Sabastian catching his breath as he was in very intense meditation. Yes I am thank you. His eyes being blood shot red. I can't help but seeing a tear drop fall from your eye. Sarah whispered. As soon as we land if you don't mind we can go get a cup of coffee if you like. No thank you very much. But I don't drink coffee or strong drinks. Well would you like to chat with me? You are welcome if you like. I don't bite. I would like to be your friend.

Sabastian being raised macho and as the one who called the shots when speaking with a woman. Had mixed feelings about this white middle age American lady calling him out to socialize. How could this be. This was unheard off in his country. Thousands of things were going through Sabastian keen alertness mind. One was the bombing of the airliners into the twin tower trade center. Was Sarah the beautiful blond lady who was inviting him for a cup of coffee an F.B.I. agent? Did he speak and look Mexican enough to pass through the Los Angeles airport gates with out being suspected as an Arab immigrant?

Fasten your seat belts. The captain of airline flight 234 yelled out to the passengers. We are going in for the landing. Sarah and Sabastian were at silence and thinking if their meeting and short conversation would have any affect when they landed on the ground. After all after the announcement of planes crashing on the twin towers had no impact on the passengers on board this flight. It was like a hoax. No one paid attention to the radios or air flight attentants and cell phones where too static because of the high air turbulance. The runway for the landing was clear as a babys butt. And the pilot got the go ahead to come on down and land. Boom!!! boom!!! squak!! squack!! streek!!! Went the 747 front landing tires. Landing accomplish and safe the captain acknowleged the tower station. Landing granted "WelCome on board" a voice from the tower spilled out.

Scores of uniformed police officers and national guardsmen were on hand. Nothing passed by them. As passengers were being escorted out one by one. The 747 was being searched from top to bottom. Every one who was of color or resembled middle eastern was being pulled over and taken for questioning. There were quite a few. Sabastian knew it was over. Sarah wanted to ask the guardsman if she could know the reason for pulling her fellow passenger's over and if she could come along. Fearing they might harrass Sabastian. But she walked slowly and dropped out of the passengers line and sneaked behind cargo to see where they were taking the detainees.

There was a large white tent on the side off the runway 9. In which all detainees where taken in there for questioning.

Looking for some one miss? A law enforcement officer comming from behind Sarah. Oh! no officer!

I was trying to get a clear picture of the runway here. My father was a captain in the airforce and told me that the runways needed to be flat dry and spotless to get safe landings. I am writing a book on landing fields that I believe could have an impact on facial cosmetics. Sure the officer responded. You can tell your whole story to the dentention center. Oh! but officer. Well ok, but you be nice to me, and don't touch me. Or I will have you fired. Oh yes? will see to this. Answered the officer.

As the officer and Sarah were walking towards the tents. Sabastian was being humilated by the guards.

Now son. Lets start over again. Don't let me lose my temper. Cryed a senior officer named the bear for his fat cheeks on his face. Now what brings you son to Los Angeles? You come to blow yourself and terrorize us? Sabastian looking lost and bewildered. Like a Sirhan Sirhan of the Robert kennedy assasination. No sir. Just came with my girlfriend. Looking at Sarah. We came on a business trip. Oh? really? Since when are Arabs allowed to mingle with American blonds? No sir I am not an Arab. I am from Mexico. Oh! a beaner huh? So a beaner with an American gringo.

No sir, you have me all wrong. My girlfriend and I were suppose to meet here in Los Angeles airport. But are flights got mixed up. She was doing business in New York and I in Texas for her. I work for her.

Oh! you do don't you. What do you do? Are you her gardener? Well I don't have to take this sir testifyed Sabastian.

So who are you? Young lady? I am Sarah the much talked about. Girlfriend of this gentleman here. Sarah being guarded by the police official on the end of interrigation table. Yes sir I am and I demand and explanation for this. I am a very important citizen of this great country. And demand a quick release of my friend and I.

Oh! now wait a second little one. Now who gives the orders here. Me or you? I do. A voice from the end of the tent cryed out. It was a tall man with a smelly Cuban cigar. And a cane to support his limping leg. The man had a strong voice much like a Teddy kennedy of the American Kennedy political dynasty family.

Please release my daughter now. I am ambassador Cunningham. And I have a letter from the president of the United States. The bear recieves the letter and makes jesters that would make a real bear meek. Well, there seems to be some mistake here sir. I am very sorry. I have to put this letter through my codes and verify from Washington D.C. Will take few minutes. Sir please have a seat. Sarah so overly joyful her father showed up. Reached over hugged and kissed him. Well daddy. She had had some shortcommings in her family with her mother. And had not been getting along with her father Mr. Cunningham. Daddy what a pleasant surprise. How is mother? Moher is fine my baby. Sarah was daddys pet. She was all he had. Sarah was Bills only child. Sarah was not Mrs. Lilys Cunninghams biological daughter. Mr. Cunningham had had an affair with a younger woman from palestine. When Bill was the ambassador to Israel. Mrs. Cunningham was in an automobile accident some time back. And lost her mother nature tenures.

Sorry Mr. Cunningham sir. Your daughter is free to go. We have orders from on high. No one is immuned from being detained. I understand officer. Replyed Bill Cunningham. Get your belongings Sarah. We have a long trip back home.

And you sir. Talking to Sabastian. You come with me. Oh! no! Sarah rebuked. He is my friend and worker. he comes with us. Well who is he dear? Remarked Bill. He is my boyfriend and best worker of my company. I send him to Mexico to do some shopping for me. And we met on the same flight. Home. After a mixed up flight.

Well if he is your worker. then get the hell out of here. But boyfriend? All these brown skins look all the same to me. Last time I remember America was a white prostestant country. Now that will be enough sir. Rebuked, Mr. Cunningham. Now you apologize to this young man. Or I will report you to your superiors. Well okay. I am so sorry Mr. Cunningham, Sarah, and you sir. Looking nasty at Sabastian.

Don't sweat sir." Sabastian replyed." We all make mistakes.

On the drive home to Palm springs. Sabastian was very thoughtful. Hoping to break away Sarah and her father. And go into hiding into a Muslim mosque someplace. But where. He didn't know the state Of Caliornia that well or at all. Someone some place who was Muslim was sure to help him out. For now this young American infidel family Sabastian thought. Was sure to help him out and get him to his distination.

So how you like working for my daughter? What was your name son? Sabastian daddy. Sarah blurred out. Sabastian sitting very quiet in the back seat of the mercedes. Sabastian sir. Sabastian Mijarez. To serve you sir.

Very polite boy. Where are your parents Sabastian? Mr. Bill Cunningham a very good driver steering like if he was a Mario Andritti type driver. California hiways were some of the worlds worst. My parents are in Mexico sir. They are very humble people. Very bad leaders and economy there. You are telling me Sarah spoke out. Mexico was suppose to rise out of its doledrums. With the new President Vicente knoxs.

Mexico was turning to Gringo last names. Many familys rich and poor were giving their children European and American names.

As driving down interstate 10 as the hiway that goes as far south and south east towards southern California and beyond. Mr. Cunningham the sixty year old ex Ambassador to Israel. Begin to reminess about his past. Years before Sarah was born. Most of his youth was spent comming down from the San Fernanado valley. His parents were immigrants from Germany right after the war. Big "Jewish penis Bill" was three years old when he arrived with his mother and father in New York. With hundreds of other immigrants from that part of the world. Most Jews and Gyptsys that did escape Hitlers holocust escaped to other neighboring countrys. Bills parents escaped to England. Then here to America. Others weren't so lucky. "Big Jewish penis Bill" was called this because when Bill was in the San fernando valley in California growing up. As a soccor star stand out. Bill needed a double size jock to cover his God given jewels. Most Jews were circumsized. Bill wasn't. And his baggy sport underwear supported it. when he competed. Sometimes Bill was so agressive. Mother nature slipped out.

CHAPTER 2

THE LONG TRIP TO PALM SPRINGS

Why so far away daddy? Sarah broke the silence as Mr. Cunningham passed a cattle of windmills across the desert as approaching a turn off that leads to Palm Springs and a underground government city with one thousand chosen world officials with all the comforts and pleasures under the Palm springs hill mountain off the main hiway one-eleven as it is called.

Oh nothing my dear. I am wondering where we can put Sabastian for the nite. A young boy like him would be under great suspicion. Considering everything that has happen this morning at the world trade center. Sabastian was keeping a low profile wondering hmself of his future. Well sir. Don't worry bout me. I am sure many Hispanics can help me out. Maybe for a nite or two.

But daddy he works for me. Sarah not staying silent. I can't go underground now. I have my business to run. I am not afraid of terror. You tought me daddy not to ever give in to fear. Sabastian and I will find a small cottage someplace to do my business to sell my cosmetics. Plus I have my company in Los Angeles. I have been so confuse with terrorist thing I forgot that I was a business owner. Good thing. Replyed Bill. Me too. I even forgot that I am a distinquish noble ambassador. Ex- ambassador to Israel. See what horror does to the human mind. It humbles us to peanuts.

Back in the seat. Sabastian very quiet and pensive. Thinking what he was going to do. Sarah seemed to like him. And this was good. He could manipulate her. And get what he wanted done so he thought. Bing a fundamentalist muslim from Egypt. Having join the Al-qaida jhad of Osama Bin Laden. When he was barely sixteen. From a humble family off ten kids. Sabastian being the one in the middle. Always got pushed around. His other brothers and sisters got jobs and became educated and mingled into the Egyptian society that was purely mythical in Islamic rituals driving many Egyptians to seek western style capitalistic and religious ideals.

You okay back there son? Cryed out ambassador William Yakob Cunningham. We are arriving to Palm Springs. My daughter wants to find a cottage for you both. Is it okay with you?

No problem sir. Sabastian very polite as he was a very eduacated and muslim fearing god person. If its okay with my boss Sarah. I welcome her decisions. Yes its okay Sabastian. Don't worry. I know awful thoughts must be going through your mind with this terror attack at the world trade center. I know many of you Hispanics resemble middle eastern folks. But don't worry we will be alright. Okay then we got a deal says Sabastian.

Fine then we will look at the chamber of commerce and see if they can accomadate you. They should have something there.

The onced sleepy resort town of Palm Springs California where great people from all over the world made their home or vacation day butes under the warm hot desert sun was changing. Where onced lush handsome homes with swimmng pools and golf courses and tennis clubs flourished. For the rich few. Is fastly becomming a multicultural community owned heaven for poor Hispanics and Gays. Big brother has also added his mark to the colorful town. There isn't a place where a hidden Camera of some kind is in stalled. You name it. In the casinos, rest rooms, parking lots, librarys, even churches. Most homes and cottages are owned by working class people. Homes like the late singers Frank Sinatras and Elvis king of rock. Presely belong to Chinese desidents where down town Palm Canyon drive. Where young college kids came to pass the easter week vacation. Was solid gays. Holding hands down the street. And leather biker gangs too.

Though Palm Springs started as a small village back in the early turn of the century. Where silent movie stars like Rudy Valentino and director Frank Capra came into town. Many more celebreties begun buying property and land here and many more came after.

Today the real big finacier shots from around the world had build an underground city under a huge mountain off Palm Springs. Possibly knowing that there was going to be terrorist backlashing across The United States and the world.

This city was to serve as the model for perserverance of a new world republic that was to emerge. The undergound city was named "A Trillion Springs". Why the name for this? No one knew. But many believed scores of astro showers were to rain in Southern California soon. astro showers you say? Maybe they meant showers from Nuclear bombs. Not the bright heavenly stars the creator created.

What ever the story to this Handsome resort town heaven onced called Palm Springs. Is really more underground now. Thousands of feet below sea level. Maybe another Lost continent of Atlantas to be buried soon?

Much of the Coachella Valley where south eastern valley is now. Was called Coachella. Becouse of the late Indian tribes who were the original inabitants three thousand years ago and called themselfs the Cahuillas. Was below a large lake of water that sprung out of the Pacific ocean through a rip from Baja California and through colorado river that poured into a salt basin that became know as the salton sea. Today the salton sea is a fresh water lake. And a Indian resort and reservation for community understanding of space aliens and ufology. The now defunct Roman Catholic church is a co-partner in this venture.

Well then here we are folk! expressed Mr. Cunningham. Nothing like having a place to rest your head. Seems like a nice little bunglo at he end of the town.

The bungulo was located about a block away from trillion Springs the underground bunker in North Palm Springs.

Well how about some dinner folks. Ahh!! thought you never would suggest daddy. I am starving. How about some submarine ham sanwiches. Thought I saw a deli over there as we were comming into town.

What would you like to eat Sabastian? Speak up my boy. You are so quiet. An old chinese proverb.

"He that is not of tongue, may never get none". Ha, Ha, Ha. Thought I would slip in that one. Ha, Ha, Ha. Daddy stop it. Now you are being naughty cryed out Sarah.

Sabastian. Being embarassed by the whole scenario. Was being talorant. Being raised strong muslim. This kind of speech was worthy of cutting out your tongue.

Well Sir. I am not to much for American food. But a good Hamburger would be nice.

You got it Sabastian. Now lets go to that deli my dear you saw at the intrance of the town.

Sitting down eating at the deli and chatting was getting boring. The conversation was just dragging on. Mostly about Sarahs business. Sabastian looked worried and bored. Sitting next to the Cunninghams in the deli were a family of bikers with tatoos. One had a snake like serpent that encircled his Eyes and curled to the center of his chest. The serpent had its tongue hanging out. And it spoke out the name. "Majic Baby".

Sabastian notice this. And got up and began walking out the door.

Were you going sissy? A voice came out of the neighboring table. Sabastian reacting angrily to himself.

One of the bikers wearing a low cut sleeveless leather jacket pulled his leg out as Sabastian was walking out and tripped Sabastian so that Sabastian went tumbling clear out the door. Gentlemen, gentlemen persuaded Mr. Cunningham. Yes!!! cryed out Sarah. What is the meaning of this? We demand an apology.

She cryed out. Sarah lets get the heck out of here.

Mr. Cunningham responded.

The owners of the deli came out in a hurry and demanded the bikers leave the deli.

The owners were a humble couple from Tihiti.

They had escaped an uprising of neonazis in their country. That said they were muslims of the aryan stock. Mr. Brando as the owner called himself. Becouse of the love of the great American egotistical actor of the "Godfather" and "A street car named desire" movie fame. Actor Marlon Brando. Came right out and demanded the bikers apologize or face his Karate experts. He had two. Ready for any kind of disobedience in his deli.

Sabastian went running to the Cunnighams automobile location and waited there for them he wasn't about to start a fight. When he had just flew away from the one fight of his life. Sabastian was prolific in the martial arts. He was the best fighter in most middle eastern countrys. In fact he beat out one of Israels best.

Excuse us sir. And we are very sorry commented the leader of the bikers group. But our buddies here haven't adjusted to nice living yet…Ha, Ha, Ha, they all laughted.

Well here you can have my lady biker. Ha, Ha, ha. No!!! just kidding the leader scoffed we are out of here. Lets ride guys. Got better places to go.

Thank you Gentlemen. Commented Mr. Cunningham. We accept your apology in behalf of our friend. Hope you have a very nice day. What ever is left of it.

We are so!! sorry sir. The owner embarassed. But trust me this will not happen again. No charge fro the food. You have very nice day and come again. Tell your friend we are very sorry and he is always welcome.

We well Mr.? what is your name? Responded Sarah. Oh! "Brando". said Lu. Lu Brando.

Good name. You any relation to Marlon Brando?

He is my hero Lu said.

Ha, Ha, Ha, He was very fine actor at one time. Don't know what happen to him well got to go. Sabastian!! Very sorry for the incident. Every thing is all taken care off here. The owner gave you some sanwiches and some other goodies. "Praised Mr. Cunningham."

Yes Sabastian I am so!! sorry for this thing.

I will make it up to you. I promise. Please don't be angry comforted Sarah. Don' t worry. Seems like this hasn't been my week. Every wrong thing has been happening to me. Sabastian replyed after managing to put on a smile.

Sabastian's faith in Islam was very strong. He wasn't like the terrorist fundamentalist that wanted to blow up the world. He knew that there was a higher supreme being that would take care of all injustices done to his faith and people in Eygpt. And the world as a whole. Islam in its true nature was a very peaceful religion. Like most religions of the world it believed in the story of Abraham and Adam and eve. As their founding fathers of earths creation.

Sabastian believed that some day the supreme being of his faith called "Allah", Would free the world of the infidels. Or non believers. And would set up an earthly paradise. Sabastian was not a too fond of the prophet Mohammad. The founder of Islam. He felted there were to many contradictions in Mohammads writings.

Sabastian was a young twenty-one year old searchin for truth. And America unlike the middle east the cradle of religious thought was going to bring him closer to his dreams.

In the cottage Sabastian was feeling kind of nervous. Mr. Cunningham had offered Sabastian a place to stay and sleep at a friends house in Palm Springs. But Sabastian decline. Sabastian thought he would chance it staying close to Sarah. Sarah not objecting to stay in the same room with a man. Especially if she had a crush on him. Knew better. Her Father always taught her to never be in the same room with a man no matter who he was.

Her father had enough confidence in Sarah knowing her daughters sex and love life were her own business. He knew Sarah did not give in easly. Especially to her own hired help.

Okay kiddos. You have a very wonderful time. Have to go to the bunker. This is my code phone number Sarah. Call me if something comes up. Ok daddy. Sabastian and I will be shopping here in Palm Springs for material for my business.

Alright sweeting have a wonderful time and Sabastian be strong and don't let anyone think you are not a free man. Those damned terrorist thugs really ruined this country. I can see. Don't worry Mr. Cunningham. I will be careful and take care of Sarah with all my heart. She is a very wonderful lady and boss. Well thank you Sabastian didn't know you thought of me as wonderful. He he he. Sarah laughed.

Sabastian playing his cards almost perfectly. Was running out of ideas. How long would it be before Sarah and Mr. Cunningham found out that he was an Eygptian that was from a terrorist group that his conscious denounced as satanic. And prefered to go it alone to take his chances as a liberated free human being. It seems to Omar his real name. That religion and cults was not what his real self was looking for he was really looking for truth. His denouncing the terrorist suicide airplane crash bombing into the twin tower buildings in New York. Proved this. He had to tell someone the truth about himself. Could he rely in Sarah? Could she be trusted?

Sabastian you worry me. Why do you space out so much? You seem to always be in another world. Do you miss your family in Mexico? Oh yes! replied Sabastian. I really love them so much. I wonder what they are doing right now. How many brothers and sisters did you say you had? and did you tell me your mother wasn't alive? I don't remember if you told me this. Maybe its a premonition. Oh, well now let me see.

Sarah do you love me? Come here now and sit down. I have something very important to tell you. well Sabastian you surprise me. Well you must think I am a loose woman picking up a young man to come to bed with me. No! no! not at all eyed out Sabastian. Well Let me see. We don't even know each other. And we are in this same cottage together. Like as we were lovers.

CHAPTER 3

THE TRUST

Sarah? "whispered Sabastian". We met unexpectly in a very strange way. I don't even know you or you me. Are you really Sarah Cunningham?

Why yes. Sabastian what are you getting at? I am sorry for not being more introductive. But when we made eyes on the airplane. I saw a great passion in your eyes. I figured you liked me. And also when we were detained at the airport and you made the call that I was your boss to the agent. I felt so attracted to you. And everything happened so fast. But here we are now. Lets really get to know each other.

That could be a hardship. Exclaimed Sabastian.

Ok, lets begin with you Sarah. Well let me see. What would you like to know? I am thirty years of age. Rich, white and the all American girl. Laughing out loud. You pretty modest responded Sabastian. In my country they would have stoned you to death. Where in Mexico? They don't have capital punishment there. No in Egypt. Said Sabastian. Egypt? What are you doing in Egypt? Thought you said you were from Mexico. You have it written all over your face. M.E.X.I.C.A.N. Laughing hilariously.

Sabastian's demeanor blushing. Like ready to explode.

Sarah. I am a proud Islamic believer that feels that he has been betrayed by my Egyptian family and countrymen. I joined a robinhood like Islamic cult that bombed the twin tower buildings. Sarah eyes concentrating straight into Sabastians eyes.

When I was sixteen I needed an escape a way out of my humble beginnings. The koran faithfully protects the rights of every family. Through my god Allah. But our leaders and holymen have made it a den of infidels and thiefs. In this cult called the Al-Qaida or the base. I met this man named Osama Bin Laden. He is a very wealthy man from Saudi Arabia. He has trained thousands of Islamic men from all over the world to destroy America mostly and countrys from the free world. This man Osama hates America and Americans. To death.

He trained us to become martyrs he says. He says if we do Allahs will. And die a martyr we will be blessed with seven virgins in paradise.

What are you tellng me, Sabastian? Sarah is confused.

I am tellng you that I denounced the AI-Qaida. I broke the oath to hijack an American airliner and crash into the Twin tower buildings. I was being trained to what you Americans call terrorisim. I hate it! I hate it! I am not a terrorist! I love my god! My name is not Sabastian! My name is Omar Bin Mohammad. Crying his heart out. Sarah reaches out to Omar and embraces him with her arms. Sarah really doesn't know to much about the Al-Qaida or Osama Bin Laden for that matter. She despises religion and everything that goes with it. She was raised Jewish but for what she knew about it was like knowing what the jewish holocust was all about. It was something from the past. Don't cry Sabastian or Omar. I still am fasinated by you. Well let it all out. Cry all you want too. Crying is really good for you. From now on. I am going to give you a bit of my own medicine. Welcome home my love. Welcome home. Poor baby you must be terrified to be here telling me all this. With no direction. Alone for all these years in hiding and running from yourself. We are going to start a brand new life. With love and gentleness. Poor baby. Welcome home. Welcome home. Sarah was really quick to be understanding. She was in love.

Omar becoming conscious of his crying on a womans breast. Much more a foreign woman. How can this be. Totally out of the question. He was a muslim macho man. Women were suppose to be subservant to man. As written in the Koran and book of Genesis old testament bible. Where it read. "And becouse Eve disobeyed Adams command not to eat the fruit of the tree of good and evil less you die". And that god would increase the pain in womans child bearing because of her disobedience. And man would rule over woman.

What was Omar doing bowing to this infidel he thought. Well all these thoughts were to go out of his mind once and for all time. He had broken the oath of the Al-qaida and the muslim faith. So what. It was time for a change. From now on he would be his own man.

Omar you ok? Honey. Don't worry bout a damn thing. I am here amd will support you in any way and form I can. I think we met in such an odd way for a reason. I am beginning to get the picture now. Lets turn on the news on the t.v. now.

I need to take care of you. We are both fugitives. You for tempting to hijack an American airliner and crash into the twin tower building in New York. And me for harboring you.

Ok now let me think. We are safe now. No reason to get histerical. Don't worry. I am not afraid of any thing. There is nothing anyone can do to me what my distiny had already done. Replyed Omar. Ok lets turn on the t.v. Look they are saying on the t.v. that four maybe five airliners crashed on American top class buildings. One was headed or the white house but crashed into an open field in the State of Pennsylvania. Oh! my god.

There was suppose to be a third plane crash below the twin tower buildings. The plane we were on. Oh Omar! I am so happy the great creator of heavens ad earth touched your ever sweet heart and made you realize that it was all wrong. In the Jewish faith you can go to hell for taking your own life. Its called suicide. I think I read it in the book of Moses. Hummm so glad we are here safe.

I am glad to Sarah. I am glad we have all that behind us now. Its time to move foward into a new life and spirit. I want to forget my past. A beautiful lady like you can make all this happen. Sarahs eyes sparkled as Omar reached out to caress her soft white pinkish face. He kisses her and holds her close to him. This truely a love made in the heavens.

Sarah I never felt this feeling in my life. There is something so beautiful here. I, I feel like a complete different person. Like something out of a fantasy.

Its not a fantasy Omar. Its you and me. Sarah confessed. I have been married before and I have felt nothing like this either. I feel so scared for us too. We have to much to live for and we have a world that doesn't appriciate love and peace.

Peace will come when people begin to realize that life was made to enjoy. Not to be better than one another. Life is so beautiful. You are so lovely my Sarah. I never met anyone like you. Perhaps it is becouse I never really gave myself a chance.

We all have this deep love inside of us all. Its like a well that we have to dig way down to fine it. "Sarah sings out". "Day after day, we must face a world of strangers were we don't belong", "we are not that strong". Let me be the one you run too, let me be the one you come too, When you one someone to turn too. "Let me be the one". Its a beautiful song. Omar whispered out. You have such a beautiful voice. I wish I knew how to sing.

My mother never tought us how. Maybe some day I will learn.

Its not that hard to sing. Well you need alot of soul. Said Sarah. I took opera in college. Here turn of the t.v. What you say we go get some chinese food. Ok? Humm ok, but lets be very cool about every thing. Lets not even mention what happen. Omar exclamed. Remember We are like Bonnie and Clyde, Ha ha, ha. Omar! you are westernize. you really know our culture. Responded Sarah. Well yes said Omar. Those of us that wanted an Education of the west had access of television and a library in Egypt. Many poor kids live on the street begging for money and alms. But I went to the library and helped clean and dust the books. The librarian gave me access to much western literature and culture. Humm, you are interesting. Tell me more about yourself. And then I will tell you bout me. Well really for being twenty- one year of age. I am really about fifty. I really feel older than my age. Omar said. Yes I think we can chat a bit.

Here, said Sarah lets go over to the north end of town. I saw a Mexican resturant there. Do you like Mexican food? Well Isn't my name Sabastian Mijarez? laughted Omar. Ha, Ha, Ha, laughted Sarah. Well of course it is Mr. Mijarez. Ha, Ha, Ha.

Be my guest.

As they bothed laughed there heads off. They knew of the dangers that awaited them if the stepped out of line. From now on Omar would be Sabastian from Mexico. To every one they encountered. But to Sarah always Omar. And Sarah would be Sarah his boss of the cosmetic company Edensrose.

As days went by. Omar alias Sabastian kept a low profile. Sarah and Omar went every where together. Almost like brother and sister. He was Sabastian Mijarez from Mexico and she was the ex- Miss Universe Miss America the daughter of a well established ex-Ambassador too Israel.

The world was changing at a rapid pace and Omar seemed to know about the changing trend of economics, religion, and social classes of the world. Sarah who herself was an activest in her college days. Had lost interest in the prophetic world do to her own personal shortcommings in her love life. Now perhaps. Omar could lift her spirits to kingdom come.

Omar the twenty-one year old was very keen and aware. But running like a fugitive would be a big challenge to him and Sarah. Sarah didn't really know the risk she was taking. Harboring a would be International terrorist what ever the out come both Omar and Sarah loved Adventure and tackling the problems of their young life to boot.

CHAPTER 4

THE VICTORY PARTY

All was peachy cool, a couple of weeks went bye with out incident. Sarah and Omar were keeping a low profile and working hard on Sarahs business.

They were together at all times.

Sarah was getting restless as she and Omar sleped together in the same room but with out mating. Omar would have it his way. When ever they were to shower and undress Omar would have the lights out or go out off the room. And respect Sarah's privacy.

Sarah followed and found the custom quite Biblical and rooted like in her ancient jewish culture. A coming thursday Sarah and Omar were invited to a victory part at the Trillion Springs undergound bunker. Many heads of state from around the world would be there. This was to be both Sarah and Omars biggest challenge of there fugitive run. The Bonnie and clyde like saga surrounded and entraped in the lions den. But Omar and Sarah hadn't done a thing to break the law. But fall in love.

Goodmornin Dr. Cunningham. A bell hop young lady speaking out to Mr. Cunningham as he was taking his usual morning swim in the facility pool.

Goodmornin Clara. How is your mother feeling?

Quite well Dr. Cunningham. She can get up and walk much better now.

Clara was a bell hop by incognito. She really was the house spy. She worked for intelligence. She had been an operations manager for the F.B. I. counter intelligence in north Africa in Lybia. Now she and her ageing mother were house guest as intelligence monitoring guest personal in the underground facility. Kinda like Hitlers S.S. Her mother had fallen down and broken her leg.

Well swell. Tell her Lalith my wife would like to have tea with her Saturday. We are Jews and our savoth is Saturday. I sure will responded Clara.

I will let her Know this afternoon. Are you comming to the victory this Thursday? I sure am wouldn't miss it for the world. Responded the Doctor. My daughter and I and her business manager.

Great! will be looking forward to celebrating with you. See you then. Goodbye, nice chatting with you Dr. bye now.

It was a cooling changing temperture in Palm Springs California. The middle days of October. The world series was about to begin. The Los Angels dodgers and California Angels had beaten the odds. They were about to face each other after so many years of rolling around like a red shirted team in the minor leagues. Los Angeles dodgers hadn't been a contender since the days of the Italian mouth. "Ken Rocher". Ken Rocher was known as "The mouth". For mouthing three world championship teams to victory. His spitting and screaming got him three rings and an induction into the hall of fame of baseball. Even the president of the United States emulated his mouth and had his lips widen in Rochers honor. This was a fact.

The Los Angeles dodgers almost had the perfect record in the National baseball league. They were batting a perfect 500 average. In turn the Anaheim angels struggled below 400 average. But managed to win games by defult into the world series.

It was early thursday morning. Sarah and Omar had gotten up early to go shopping at the local mall. There was a grocery store that carrried all the green vegetables any one would want. Sarah loved Romain salads and Coachella Valley artichokes. They reminded her of the artichokes of The holy land. Jeresulem. She loved them. With sour cream made from goats milk.

Omar on the other hand loved artichokes grown in Eygpt. But considered eating them with goats sour milk ungodly. He thought the goats milk was sacred. And should be drunk sweet and warm on holy days. In respect to founding father Mohammad. Who he believed left on a unicorn to heaven. The unicorn resembling the family of the goats and rams much alike.

Oh! it's so nice in this store. Its like an open market. Look how much variety of fruits and vegetables they have in here Omar. Sarah lanced out. Yes indeed. Quite lovely. Ummmm reminds me of the open markets in. "OOP'S"; Sorry, well. Lets just say it is beautiful. Omar speaking in a low tone of voice. The open market was a bit crowded. People from all over the world. Sarah cought on. As to what Omar was going to say. The open markets in Eygpt. Ha, Ha, Ha. Sarah laughted out loud. "know what you mean my dear". In a humorus type of twitch in her voice. Something commedian Woopie Goldstern my say.

Well as Sarah and Omar were trying to figure out what to buy. Two funnie looking looking objects were hidden between the produce. Omar cought on. But Sarah was a little slow this time. Omar pulled her hand and walked away from the isle of produce and stood on a corner of the ice machine to the side of the produce and cautioned Sarah about the video cameras on the produce section. Sarah didn't notice. But thanked Omar.

Thank you Omar. That was a close call. Let me catch my breath. You have such a strong crip in your hands. I thought you were freaking out here lets buy a soft drink from this machine. Do you have fifty cents on hand. No! No! wait its one dollar???? Oh well. Here I can afford it said Omar. I have two dollars and fifty cents. Ha, Ha, Ha. You haven't given me my allowance telling Sarah kiddenly. Oh well Omar. Tonite at the victory party you will be holding all my credit cards. Everyone must know you are my right hand man and fiancee.

Lavishly and shining Omar and Sarah managed to get dressed and look their very best for the party. Sarah was wearing an ordinary summer skirt and blouse with high heel. Nothing fancy so not to cause attention to her and Omar. Sarah did not need any type of fashion any way. She was very sexy and attractive in all clothe. Also she would wear very mosdest jewlery. A simple bracelett.

On the other hand. Omar bought a simple medium dark suit with tie and white shirt. No cufflings. To pass as a normal American of Mexican desent. That wasn't after Sarah's money.

He would be Sabastian Mijarez the business manager of Sarahs cosmetic company.

Sarahs father Bill, would have the shadow government limosene pick them up. Her father would have it no other way. Security would be tight. Omar was scared to death. Counceling with Sarah to let him stay at the cottage alone. Sarah wanted Omar to attend for business reasons. And Sarah wanted Omar to confront the shadow crowd as her philosophy to overcome the fear and the suspicions of any who might question who Omar is. Sarah felt that sooner or later Omar and she had to confess as to who Sabastian really is and to Sarahs love affair with him.

It was a perfect night. Palm Springs boulivard was packed with tourist and locals. They had a gay and lesbian festival and a motor cycle gang riding their choppers up and down the strip.

The college kids were no competition to the down trotted of yesteryear. The gays and biker kind were the incrowd these days. A lot of the old customs were gone. There were also alot of Jehovas witnesses handing out the tower magazine about the comming paradise to earth for Jehova god. There were also muslims protesting terrorism and the American government.

This was not to bother Omar and Sarah for they were way beyond what they would come to consider "simple" politics of the common people. Although these kind of politics were their bread and butter and the money that went into their bank account. Oddly enough who could want more payouts. To be free and sound is all Omar and Sarah desire.

Even the limo Sarah and Omar were to ride in was being escorted by motor cycle buffs. These gang members preyed on the rich to show society they were very charitable. So they had four black leather bikers and their women escorting the limo to its destination.

The limosene ride to Trillon Springs was nervousness for Omar but for Sarah it was high class. Sarah couln't wait to shine at the party as she had attented many diplomatic functions with her father and step mother in her past. After all her father was the ex- Ambassador to Israel.

A little smile of her grin and a yes sir and no mam was all her speech was needed for this high society crowd. Sarah had instructed Omar who had never attended such galas to just be himself. Outside his believes how could Omar be himself. If he never attented high society functions in Eygpt. Much less here in America. After all he would be like the Zorro or a Robinhood in disquise. After all he was a would be one of the most wanted torrorist in the world. Omar Bin Mohammad was the son of a humble Egyptian family turned cultist in a so- called Muslim fundamentalist ring. Runned by infidel thugs that had nothing todo about the true Islam faith. Who wanted to destroy the United States of America and their allies. Omar had his work cut out for him. There were to be muslim dipolmats at the victory party too. Muslims against terror who dealt on business only with the western nations.

The lions den

As the limo and the biker escorts approached the Trillion Springs underground shadow government bunker. Scores of national guard troops were on hand. You would think it was an army camp. Omar eyes popped out as Sarah held his hand as to say don't worry, "I love you". And we will go through this unnotice.

Omar had forgotton how to pray. Usually before a confrontation muslims would give thanks to their god. This time he never even thought of prayer. All he could think about was "Am I crazy or what". He thought I avoided a suicide crash for my life. Now I am going to blow myself up again? Oh! what the brothers in the Al- Qaida would give to be me now. This is Al-Qaidas dream. To crunch the American infidels In their own safty haven. But is it? I would be sittiing at the right hand of the prophet Mohammad. With many virgins. Peace be on to him. But no. This is not my way. I am a free man. I don't belong to any religious group or believe any more. I am an American. Or at least I want to be. I love Allah and the prophet Mohammad. But there has to be more to life than living in fear and war with the world. If Allah was all mercifull. Then why does he allow greed and war amongs the nations. Something is wrong.

The hells Angel biker stepped aside as the limosene driver opened the door for Sarah and Omar. -alias Sabastian-. I hope you enjoyed your trip to the bunker Miss Cunningham. Oh! you know my name. "Replyed Sarah". Oh! yes. Didn't you know? I was one of the youngest chauffers at capitol hill when your father was ambassador.

Humm, don't remember must of been to young myself. Said Sarah. Yes you were miss Cunningham. If I remember correctly, You were just nine. I was a young intern learning the trades.

Mack was a white anglo saxon protestant who wanted a government job way back then when the old George Fuller or forty -one as he became known. Was president back then...Mack wanted to be the white house chaplin. But lost his faith in a sailing trip in the bermuda triangle. He believed he had gone back in time and seen Jesus Christ crucified pleading with the jews that he wasn't the messiah. Mack was something else. He was the resurrections answer to Omars seven virgins in paradise.

Alright great. You have a nice evening and here is my card. When you are ready to leave the party. Just show my card to the desk clerk at the front office. He will call me to pick you up and take you home. Thank you! Ah your name is Mack? It says here in the card. "Yawned", Sarah. Yes mam. Mack the knife. No! just kidding. I am Mack Mcdugule. Its a french name…Ha, Ha, Ha. Ok fine. You have a nice eveing and we will call you when we are ready to go home. Right Omar? Oh! yes by all means Miss Sarah.

Omar knew he had to put on the act of his life. When he was in Eygpt he used to go to theaters and act that he was Al Pacino the famous Italian Actor from New York. Every one in the Egyptian Ghettos loved Al Pacinos crazy characters. Especially the one in "Scarface". Where he personafied a troubled Cuban refugee that came to America ninety miles on rafts and tire tubes across the Ocean from Castros, Cuba Island prisons. They were called "The marilitos".

As Sarah and Omar approached the mountain called Trillion Springs. There was no door. Or entrance. It was off something like off the twilight zone. As many dressed elegant people approached the mountain people would disappear off the bright clean air and appear inside the mountain guest room. Many guest would assemble there get their Identification cards checked out. Before entering into the main hall. The lazer codeing device would light on your body and person to see if you had any weapons or were any couse of danger before entering. The lazer checked out your rna dna code to see if you were nervous or a threat to security inside the bunker.

As soon as Omar entered the compound. Red lights went on. Security was waiting for him.

What is the problem sir? I am a guest of Bill Cunningham and her Daughter Sarah. I am an employee of Sarah's cosmetic company.

Just routine check sir. Repyed the chief security officer. May I see your credentials please? Here you are sir. I can assure you I am a legal resident in America. I Have student diplomatic credentials from Mexico country. And was hired by Miss Cunningham to manage her business of cosmetics. Replyed Omar. Ok have a nice evening replyed the chief officer. Sorry for the inconvience. Pass on through.

This was a shock to Omar. If this was that easy to get through this high tech operation any one could lie their way in through.

The entrance was Sarahs happiest nite. Now on to the guest rooms and a nite to remember. Well good evening Sarah a government offical greeted Sarah. Hows the business moving along? Well find Mr.? I didn't catch your name? Bullard. Jim Bullard.

Nice to meet you sir. Sarah and Omar proceeded on to the quest rooms.

Every one in the bunker seemed so friendly and courtiest. Like something out of a rehabilitation center. Sarah had been to a place of alcoholism with her ex- husband of three years. Seemed he hit rock bottom and decided to live his own life instead of being sober with Sarah.

But this place here underground was more exciting. The place was like a palace. Red carpet and all. How you like it so far Omar? Sarah whispered to Omar. Omar was in another world. Like an electronic mail reading every angle of the place.

Just find honey. How are you doing? Honey? Oh! lashed out Sarah. Your so! darling. I am moved by your sweet words. I didn't think you had it in you. At least in this place. Ha, Ha, Ha, laughed Omar. I guess when the tough gets going. The best comes out in me. Hummm I like that Omar. It so sexy. Sexy? what is that? Omar replyed down rightly. Omar? your being silly now. Lets go in that room and get a cold drink.

Sarahs father Bill did not show up to meet them at the entrance. Sarah did not seem to mind. She was going to have a wonderful time. And perhaps thought that daddy was busy with his long time friends from the government. Besides Sarah didn't want any embarassments or intrutions in her and Omars life. After all they were fugitives. Wanted dead or alive by the most powerful government of the world. And after all they were inside their hide away. Talking about returning to the scene of the crime?

Hi, dear. A voice came out of the guest room. Well hello dad. How are you? We missed you at the entrance. Omar got pulled over but it was taken care off soon. Oh yes my dear. I am so sorry. I was detained at a conference for the Israeli leaders it was a peaceful conference. Just politics etc, etc. Well! glad we found each other daddy. Here lets have some champane and toast to our wonderful future in the twlight zone. Ha, ha, ha. Twilight zone is about what we are living these days with all this terror going on well lets not chat bout that. And enjoy our selfs. Growled! ambassador Cunningham.

Good thing lashed out Omar. Lets take a look around the compound. Are we allowed? Sure we are I am here said Bill. And where is mother Lilith? Aroused Sarah.

Humm mother decided not to attend Sarah. She went to a friends house outside the bunker. Your mother is so suspicious. She thinks the govenment is full of a bunch of wackcos. Can you imagine. She thinks the real terrorist are our own leaders. And the suicide bombers are nothing more than robots. Cryed out Mr. Cunningham. Hummm wonder what she meant by that.

Look! Omar suggested. Why don't we visit that room there! It looks like a space station. Well we can only view the room from the windows ouside Omar. Even I, Have no pull and permission to go in there. The underground shadow goverment compound was like something out of an old Orson wells movie. It was like a huge observatory palace with all the accomodations any civilized person would want. Unlike the caves of the Al-qaida in Afgahnastan. This was like a space odyssey. A first class into the future world. And it wasn't make believe. It was all now. And a plan for the worlds very elite to take over the world.

Enough of the politics and lets have some fun. What do you say we go dancing. Expressed Bill. Oh! great yes. Is there a disco tech here or country western? Sarah sung out. feel like dancing. Hmmm I believe there is one over there.

Back into those doors. Well how would you know Omar? I have extrasensory perception. Ha, ha, ha. well maybe you are right Omar lets go find out.

There down a hall way into the east wing was a large entertainment room. They called it Atlantis passage song room. Why they would call this is any ones guess. Nothing was ever known about the lost continent of Atlantis. If this was what the orchestrators named it for.

Inside the large dancing hall was an open protective glass dome as the sealing of the roof. A skylite. You could see the stars of the heavens above. Nothing could penitrate through germs bacteria, nuclear chemicals etc. Lazer lights glowed all over the room with glitter falling from the sky. As if they were meteors.

They had five bars and food concessions all around. It had three stages with different types of music. In the center stage there was disco in the left stage there was country music and in the right stage punk alternative music. They had a second floor with a pyramid like theater on center stage. And a huge black glittering diamond with enscriptions writing across it. It read:

"THE GREAT ARCHITECT OF THE UNIVERSE".

Oh! How gorgeous sniffed Sarah. Want to be here all night. Lets dance Omar. What? Omar rejected. Oh! Forget who you are sniffed Sarah. Life is to short to be passive. Ok you asked for it twitched Omar. Omar let go and took Sarah by the hand and went to the middle of the disco floor. Heavy techno music was being played. Mr. Cunningham also went to the dance floor. Some young girl asked him to dance and off he went. Aha, ha, ha. This is so much fun, Omar. Haven't danced like this since my high school Graduation. And you are not doing so bad yourself. Laughed Sarah over joyfully.

Don't know were Omar got his dancing moves but, he was jumping and turning like a break dancer he must have seen many news clips in Egypt. Omar never thought of himself as a western dancer. Back home they were tought that it was satanic. But this wasn't satanic. It was fun. Aha, ha, ha, ha Omar laughted and leaped with joy. He was prespiring heavily. Omar had lost all his nervousness and was becomming another person. The dance hall was becomming packed with many middle age and young teenagers. All from families of world over dignitaries. Mr. Cunningham was not doing so bad himself. as he too was holding his ground with a pretty redhead not more than twenty four years of age.

Omar and the Cunningham family are having a wonderful time. Up stairs behind the cameras is a big brother group monitoring the dance hall. They are monitoring Omar and Mr. Cunningham very closely. They go by the names of eunuchs. There's eunuch one, two, and three monitoring the dance floor. They are one woman and two men. These three are shadow government employees that report all suspicious activity to the commission. The shadow governments commission is made up of seven men and five women. There is a thirteen member reserved for Sundays only. He is the head of the governing body. He is never seen any where. Many believe he travels to other underground bunkers around the world. Some believe he could be the third great ruler envisioned by the great seer Nostrodumus. That was to appear at the world seen to bring peace to the whole world. If he was. Well he had better do it soon. The world was at the brink of total annihiliation.

There was so much glitter in this dance hall. it would dwarf Hollywood premiers. There was so much glamour and money people with such apparel. Pretty young women and macho males with tuxidos a la sexsual. Sarah and Omar seemed like third world parties compared too the crowd. But that didn't bother Omar and Sarah. Their riches and luxury were in their hearts.

Ahhhh wow! lets rest a minute. Come lets get some refreshments guys. huffed and puffed Sarah. Yes lets do. Overly breathing was Dr. Bill Cunningham. Haven't had that much exercise since world war two. Ha, ha, ha. Well, I have been telling you to join the golf club here in the Trillion Springs daddy. Its good for you. You are almost seventy years old. Never you mind honey pie. Don't you worry bout me. I get plenty of exercise.

And I do too. With a large release of edreline Omar rushed out. I feel like I am so free. I love this place. Its like being in heaven. How would you know about heaven asked Bill? I have heard about those Crazy Mexican fiestas. Must those hot Mexican senoritas that make it heaven hey? That must be it! Laughed Omar. No! its Sarah! I am so! in love with her! Yelled Omar.

Sarah and Omar out of reality knowing they had to tell daddy Cunningham sometime soon that Omar was not a Mexican nor Sarahs cosmetic business manager. How could they do it. Well not tonite. It was a freedom of Speech and spirit victory party.

FIRST LOVE

CHAPTER 5

FIRST LOVE

The victory party was just illuminating the night.

Bill had a meeting one mile below ground level down trillion springs mountain about some terrorist connection. Sarah and Omar alias Sabastian want to party all nite long. The fear and anguish about their identity had subsided and laughter and happiness was in the air.

When you walked into the top level of the bunker.

It is if you were in some shopping center. No one could ever suspect it was a secret shadow goverment hide out of course they had the disco and shopping stores to go too. They have a medical facility at ground level. This was all something like out of a James Bond movie. George Orwells book "Nineteen-eighty-four", was surley here. But Sarah and Omar were not concerned about modern science of politics. They were deeply in love with moment by moment as the two kids in the neighborhood from across the street.

Oh so!! sweet it was. Mr. Cunningham had to go back to see his wife. Who did not want to live in the bunker compound. But bought the late comedian Bob Hope's home in pearl drive in Palm Springs just a few miles down. But not till after the ground level meeting.

Daddy, Sabastian and I have some business to attend too. We are going to get lost for a while. We shall meet you for a late dinner at Trillion Springs resturant. Ok? Hummm ok. I need to go check up on your Mother anyway later on. What do you say.

we meet at the resturant around midnite? Thats great daddy. We are going into Palm Springs to check out the town. Ok fine. Mr. Cunningham kisses Sarah on the cheek.

Sabastian, you are in charge now. Take good care of Sarah. And we'll meet you later. You have all my security and word that sarah is in good hands "Mr. Cunningham," Sir. Sabastian replyed.

You are a good man, "Mr. Cunningam," answered back". Now away with you kids.

Bye daddy. She reaches over and kisses him and hugs him.

Mr. Cunningham had great pride in his daughter. He knew when all was well. He couln't be bothered now with family problems for he had to go to a very important meeting one mile down to ground level in Trillion Springs shadow goverment. What could this meeting be about? The last time he was called for such a meeting was when he was ambassador to Yisrael. Was he really that important still to be called upon to attend such a meeting?

As Sarah and Omar were being driven down into Palm Springs. Sarah had a great eye of passion look for Omar. Moments of blushing and sensuality came across her face. Omar had given up the nervousness and was enjoying the warm clean air of the desert as they had the windows of the limosene cheauffered luxury car wide open.

Sarah's face looked liked a tigeress in heat! "Omar," "she whispered". Frantically. I want! You!

Lets go to the condo and make LOVE!

Sarah! Shame on you! It is forbitten by my faith and I must be loyal to your father "Bill Cunningham". I don't care! Sarah responded. Holding his hand with a Military grip. It was obvious who was the agressor in this relationship. Well "Ok". But don't be so forceful. Are you sure you want to make love? Or you want to have sex? Which ever comes first. I don't care. Sarah "Passioned out". Love! becomes sex and sex ends up loving. Ha, ha, ha! Well this is a matter of opinion. Omar cryed out! lets not get into this religion stuff! Sarah jolted! Driver stop! at that liquor store over there I want to buy something! Sarah yelled out!

The driver pulled over as Omar was becomming confused and side tracked from his warm desert air breese drive.

Why are we stopping here? asked Omar. We are going to celebrate tonite. I am buying a bottle of spirits. What do you drink? Oh! you don't drink. I fogot! Well I do! Sarah jumpng out of the limo excitedly. What has gotton into you? Sarah get back here! Said Omar. This is bad behavior!

Sarah running into the liquor store with her brown leather purse she had bought in Texas while buying cosmetic products for company. Searchin inside of it to see if her money was in it. Being inside the store she voiced out! Liquor man! Get me a bottle of your best scotch!

You go it lady! The liquor attented man a short, white middle aged albieno with a bald head. We have the very best! Scotland yard Scotch whisky from Scotland! its seventy dollars a bottle. The liquor man answered. Bring it down my man! and I will have some monchies to go with it and a couple of limes. And a ice bag. Great you got it! The Liquor man rushing to get the order out! Heres a Benjamin bill and keep the change! Ah! well how nice of you sweet lady! You have a very nice eveing. Sarah could become very seductve with money. She was a millionares many times over now that her company had become very successful. Rushing out to the limo she directed to the limo driver to step on the gas. And to get down the road.

Whats your name driver? Sarah trying to catch her breath. Mack! Oh! Mack the ripper. No! mack the knife! I Almost forgot all about you! My dear! How you been? thanks for comming back to pick us up. Sarah breathed out. Its quite all right my lady. Just doing my job. Mack was the lost intern that was trying to get a job in the white house as a chaplin. When the old George forty-one Bush was in office. Mack thought he had gone back to the time of the resurrection of Jesus Christ! I Through a time warp below the Bermuda Triangle.

How was your eveing at the Trillion Springs?

Just great Mack. Sorry you couldn't come in. They have a very nice disco palace there. I heard about it. Replyed. "Mack". I went in once to deliver a message. I got a glimsed. Ok here we are. Home sweet home. Thank you very much Mack. Sarah prespiring from head to toe. Here darling Sabastian. You haven't said a thing all nite. Pay Mack and lets make some sweet love! Omar exceedenly embrassed. Took out a fifty dollar bill and showed Sarah that he could be as generous as she. Wow!!!! You are a big spender Sabastian! Sarah lashed out! Ha, ha, laughed Mack! Here keep the change! Mack! Thank you very much sir. You are welcome. "Alias", Sabastian replied. Now lets go and get this young lady to bed! Oh you are going to put me to bed? That will be the day! screamed! Sarah.

Thank you all so! much! have a very nice eveing. Call me if you need anything kids I will be close bye. Mack the knife putting his tip money in his custom made zipper leather wallet.

As mack drives off. Sarah slips her key into the door key hole. She walks in and turns on the air condition to a comfortable temperture. Omar goes to the kitchen and gets a glass of milk from the refrigerator. Omar doesn't drink or smoke or drink any soda with caffine or coffee for that matter. Then he walks over to the restroom and closes the door. Honey! walk are you doing in the restroom! Sarah yelled out. Well what does every one do when they go to the restroom! "Omar", "laughed."! Ha, ha, ha. Okay but don't fall in. Ha, ha, ha you can hear Omar from the outside. Omar had just went to wash his face in the kitchen sink. Omars muslim faith forbit any seemed action of hygiene actvity around an unmarried or married female. As Sarah came out of the rest room. She began to make herself a drink. A scotch and water on the rocks would be a good drink with a lime twist. So! here we are Sarah goes over to put on a cd disk of romantic latin jass music by Gato Bravado. Hummm what kind of music do you like Omar? Sarah is calling Sabastian by his real name at these times. As she is wickedly drinking down the lush watery rye whisky scotch drink. I perfer silence. Omar wanting to get his composer together and relaxing. Oh! baby! don't be a party pooper. And come hold me close to you! Ok?

"Well.," Ok! But I am not going to bed with you!

Omar;" reached out". His hands like a Muslim that he was. I believe in the merciful and compassionate one! This kind of behavior we are in is sin! Now come on! Sarah cryed out what is sin! Who says that a little fun is wrong! Well if god did not want us to have a little fun. It would have never made a man and a woman. Yes, but not to disgrace his will. Omar, prayed out. What will? Thy will be done, on earth as it is in heaven? As the prayer goes? You can say that Omar cryed out. But the all merciful has a plan for all mankind! What about all the the religions and faiths? We have Toas, Buddhaist, atheist, the Indians, hinduist, and on and on. How can you say your god is the only one for all gods creation! I don't know! Omar breaks down on his knees and begins to cry out loud like a child! I really don't know who I am to tell you the truth Sarah! I am so! confuse! I really don't know who I am anymore. I was raised to honor the great prophet mohammad. Gods true messenger. May he be in peace. But Mohammad is in another dimention Omar. He has no power to Guide you! All of mans teachings have divine revelations but also many flaws. We are all humans! And all of the worlds religions are man made.

Yes! you are so right Sarah! Maybe I'v been such a fool! Mans interpertation of my religion has brought so much pain and torture to my people. it has made me proud and arrogant! In my country Eygpt that is suppose to be one of the most civilized countrys in the Arab world. Has so much abuse of human rights! Women get killed for no reason. Men rule like a bunch of beast! Mohammad made it very clear that women have rights to share knowlege and work and help the house hold. And all men have a right to lifes basic libertys and the persuit of happiness. Like here in America! It is true that no religion or philosophy on earth is perfect. But we must all live in peace!

Now I went and was brainwashed by an infidel terrorist. And tryed to ram an American airliner into the world tower builiding with many innocent lifes to kill. What do I do now? Even though my god given conscious said no, don't do it. I didn't do it. I feared my god and the commandment "Thou shall not kill". As we also believe in the "Ten commandments". So I broke the Al-qaidas oath and decided to take my chances and make a run for Mexico. Now I am wanted as a fugitive by the whole world! But I Don't care! Omar gets off his knees laughing.

"I do not care becouse I am a free man!" Omar begins hopping around the room like a nut. I owe no one this moment a damn thing! I have never hurt one in my life! and I never will!. "Calm down Omar." Sarah sipping another low ball glass of scotch. Don't freak out on me now! No! Sarah! I want to thank you for opening up my eyes. I am beginning to see the light. We are just humans. We are not gods or saints or anything! I have a right to love you the way you love me. Now your talking! Come down here and sit next to me on this big water bed." Sarah slurring her words. "Like if she was the great late actress "Mae West". What mommie wants, mommie gets! and baby I want you! Ok! Hey! I like the way you been calling me by my orginal name." Omar'. Omar exceedingly over joyfull! Wait let me go brush my teeth and shave! No!!!! I like you with your overnite shadowy beard. You look sexy that way. Like a real hunk! But you can go brush your teeth and take a shower! I want you fresh and clean like a baby. In the mean time I will wash and fresh in up a bit with my perfumes and tolchs too. Sarah and Omar had requested a double bed. But now the tide had changed and love was in the air. Or was it sex and passion.

Its ten-thirty in the eveing. Omar comes out stark naked singing an old rollingstones song." You can't always get want you want. But if you try sometime you might find you get what you need". By this time Sarah was stark naked under the white slicky sheets. With her legs crossed sittin up with her back agains the pillows that were backed against the wall. She had her beautiful white pinkish creamy breast covered. Where all you could see was from cleaverage up. Omar didn't seem to care what he looked like. Oh! My! What a man! For a twenty -one year old. Once a man always a man. Omar breathed out! Omar sleps under the sheets and goes for Sarahs arms and kisses her.

Sarah follows through and unfolds her long sexy theighs. And streches her body flat on her back.

Oh! baby! I've had wanted you for so! long! Sarah streched out. Humm you are so! Hot!. Omar seemed like a teeny bopper on his first date. He didn't know a thing about kissing. Honey! is this your first time? Sarah whispered in his ear. Yes. I am a virgin. A virgin! Oh! My! Alleluyia! Just a baby! Don't worry honey I will be good to you. Just relaxed. You seemed very tense and nervous. I won't bite. Just calm down. Hum, I am beginning to love you so much more! Ahhh you taste so sweet!

Here give me your tongue. This is called French kissing. French kissing? That is! Oh! never mind. Ummm I think I like it. Omars tongue was being swallowed like a candy bar. Omar loved it!

Oh!! my tongue! This hurts Sarah! But I like it said Omar. French kissing is when your tongue and mine meet. You or I can either tinkle each other with our tongues and let them find their way around in a sexy motion. Or we can just have passion play. snuggled Sarah. I don't understand. Besides it hurts. I just want to hold you close to me Omar said. He was like a frighten rabbitt. Very cold and shaking. This was his first time ever. He began to have thoughts of grandeur.

My god! This is so nice! But I am afraid if we go further into sexuality. Why Omar. Don't be afraid I will take care of you. Sarah was thirty years of age and had had various affairs. After all she had been married before. Omar to her made her feel like the shy innocent virgin girl that won the miss America beauty pagant back when she was just starting out in life. She was a young twenty-one year old who could have any man on the face of the earth. A young cocky lawyer took her for a ride and lost her viginity and innocence. Did Sarah want to do the same to Omar? Many wonderous thoughts were also going through Sarahs consciousess mind. Her life and her good name were also at stake here. After all she was voted the roll model for her American contribution to keep chastidy among the younger generation.

Omar. Tell me someting. Am I desiring to you? Why yes Sarah you are very beautiful and compassionate woman. In my country women of your caliber very snobs. They would never look at a person like me. So okay. I know you don't believe in premarital sex. And neither do I. But would you consent to having a sibling with me? Oh! Sarah. For that we need to be married. We will get married. Omar I love you! You are so different from anyone on this planet. You are one of a kind. I want to have a baby with you. A baby boy. what would you say? Omar I am part Arab. I am palestinian. Its a long story but my mother was palestinian. So don't be afraid of me. I am like you. What? really? You don't look? Omar boyishly remarked. And About the baby boy. But there is so much violence and crime for a young child to come into this world. We'll take our chances Omar." Sarah contested." Supposely the whole world lost billions of lifes in a catastrophy. We would still need people to carry on. And our chances the right conditions could save lifes. And our family would survive. You are correct Sarah.

Omar follows his male instincts and begins his journey of mother nature pouring out all of his passion and love on Sarah. The room is very dark and quiet and the outside darkess is like the sounds of silence in a warm desert summers heat of the nite. The groans and moans of two opposite worlds passionately loveing each other skin to skin and bone to bone. And a third person in the making. Perfectly being created to bring about future destinys. A marriage with out law or doctrine it was the love and spark of truth and life in the works.

In the early morning hours about 7a.m. There is a phone ring across the romantic fragrance that breesed across the room of The newly weds. Weds? At least in mother natures natural habitat.

Ah, goodmornin! Yes Who is this? Daddy! Ah! why are you calling so early in the morning! Sarah? Sarah! I have some bazar news honey! The voice of big daddy Bill Cunningham could be heard. What is it daddy? How is Sabastian? Well he is sleeping. Omar is sound asleep and snoring. Yes? Did Sabastian hurt me? Daddy! What are you saying! We are in love! We have a "BIG' SURPRISE FOR YOU! Well ok! come over around 11 a.m. daddy. should be up and going by then. Sarah 'Yawning" responded. Can you give me a hint as to what is going on? No better yet I will wait till you come.

By then Omar awakes. What is it honey! Who is on the phone? Sarah hangs the phone, it was daddy and he was acting kind of strange. They both embrace and kiss each other and roll over and fall asleep for a couple of more hours.

As they sleep its an early sunday mornin and the still of the early day seems very pleasant outside. Palm Springs had been known as a peaceful resort small village town for many years.

But for Mr. Bill Cunningham the day was a nightmare.

11a.m.

Knock! knock! The sound of hard wooden door sounded as if was a solid brick. Yes! wait a minute! We are making coffee for me and a glass of milk for Sabastian! Knock! knock! knock! The boom on the door went again. Sarah looks out the peep hole. Yes it was her daddy. Come in daddy! what is the rush? Oh! what a lovely glorias morning! Sarah stepping outside in the clean fresh air. Mr. Cunningham suspicious of Sabastian alias. Takes Sarah by the hand and pulls her out of the bungulo behind a large grapefruit tree. Trying to hang on to his cane. What daddy? Don't fall. What is the problem? Omar comes rushing out suspicious and speaks out. Is everything all right? Yes Sabastian or what ever! Mr. Cunningham regathers his thoughts. Just a family conference. We will be with you in a minute.

What is it daddy? Sarah half awake. last nite in ground level we were shown a film on torrorism. I saw Sabastian or who ever he is! standing next to Osama Bin Lade He is not Sabastian. He is Al-Qaida terrorist! Daddy he is a baby. Daddy you must be hullucinating! Baby my ass! No! dear! "Studdering I had my glasses on! and I would swear on my mothers grave. It was that man in there dressed in military fatiques!. Ok! daddy. wait here. I will be right back! No! better yet. No! yes wait here. I will tell you when to come in the house.

Stepping into the condo. Omar! Omar dear. The time has come. Daddy saw you in a Al-Qaida documentry. We been had! Now we must explain to daddy what really happen. The time has come!

Come in! daddy! Mr! Cunnigham looking bewildered and feeling shakin. Is it safe? cryed out "Bill." Why! yes daddy. Will you stop being normal. Omar! This is alias Sabastians real name daddy. And forgive us for the misleading introduction of his person. But here. Close the door behind you. We have a long and trust worthy story pure guts and con to tell. This is just like the Holocust stories you used to tell me as a child daddy.

Now were do we begin. May I introduce Omar Bin mohammud. He is one of the ten children of a humble Eygptian farmer from Cairo Eygpt. You know the country where the hebrew nation spent four hundred years as servants the good book says. Well Omar, his real name is no different that thousands of people from America and the world over! Who are looking for freedom! "Omar". Speak for your self honey! Take the floor.

Omar exceededling nervous and very embarassed. His hands together as like a rabbi or christian priest might be lecturing. Well sir. I am so sorry! I misinformed you! Mr. Cunningham. In my country they would have cut off my tongue for this. I just might do this! You crazy kid! Daddy stop it! right now! No! sir listen to me! Omar kneels on the floor and kisses 'Bills" feet! I am just a poor servant from Egypt who was looking for a way out of poverty and abuses from my country. Many of us believed America was the main reason for the Arab nations losing their religious freedom and livelihood. I am not a terrorist! I was brainwashed. Loneliness and desperation can draw a person insane! Please! listen to me sir!

Tears begin to fall down Omars brown rosey cheeks. Sir! Two years before September 11. I was recruited from the streets of Cairo. I was on my way to a pharmacy to buy my father some medicine. When I was approached by a couple young men. They were not Eygptians. They were from Saudi Arabia. They offered me much money to help my family. If I would go to one of their meetings. I did. The meeting had to with infidels betrayel and abuse of Islam. And as muslims we had to defend our soverienty of our all merciful God and religion. Well to make a long story short. "More tears running down his eyes." Sarah standing by his side holding her breath and emotions in suspense. I ended up being recruited to the deserts and hills of Afganistan without my parents knowing my whereabouts. Hundreds of young Arabs were recruited. All paid for!

At the Al-Qaida camps. Those of us who had more education than others. Were tought gorrilla warfare and high techonolgy war stragedy. I was one of the ones that learned fast. and was chosen to be a commander. Yes! Omar. Take your time son. "Bill", Changing his attitiude towards poor Omar weeping like a lost child. Here why don't we sit on the couch over here. Its funnie but what ever you are trying to tell me. "I am believeing you". Thank you sir! Please! let me go on.

To make a long story short. I volunteered to take the operation of standing by for what ever action was to be taken. But the jihad warriors did not know that the operation was to crash into the twin towers. Till the very last moment. Including myself. When it was learned. I felt an uneasiness about the operation. Most of us thought we were going to hijack the planes and the passengers as some form of protest. Then return back to the middleeast. Ok! Omar I got the picture! Don't say no more. I am a man of conscious. Now! We are all fugitives! For some reason I believe you are innocent son. I have been around liars and thgs all my life. Bu I believe you. Say no more. We have a big task ahead of us. Namely. We need to disappear and escape. It won't be long before they find our identies as the suspects. I hope know one heard us outside or around here.

Sarah and Omar we need to make plans! I have a good one. Listen up! first of all we need to change our looks. Through surgery. What! Sarah remarks. Yes! I have an old friend of my parents from the holocust days. He is eighty years of age. He worked on many people of all races disfiguring there faces and body parts to make them look like someone else. Sarah should know about this having studied cosmology. Once we look like some one else we get fake passports. They are easy to obtain. Then go live in some country were they offer ammesty.

But we can't waste any time! what about my business daddy? What about my money! I worked so hard for it! Never mind your money! We take only what we can and move on! Let the business run itself. Who did you leave as a beneficiary? No one! Sarah replys. Ok. But you were anbassador to the holy land. What can possiably they do to you daddy? Don't be so sure my dear. I am not going through the whole red tape to get a pardon! What is at stake here is you and Omar! Omar especially. I can't see him having a desent trial any where. Here in America or the middleeast! Now we have to work fast. What about mother? Sarah cautioned. Your mother never loved me dear! She has plenty of family here and in Israel. We are leaving her behind.

CHAPTER 6

FUGITIVES AT LARGE

Down on the old fairfax district in west Los Angeles. Lived Gad. Gad was an old German Jew who worked for the Nazis in world war two. But until things got bad he quit and defected into England and worked at his profession. He was a horse surgeon. He fixed lamed horses for the third Reich. He was actually pretty good. And knew just what to do. He later worked helping people.

Especially Jews who changed their physical features and wanted to stay in Germany. becouse of the good Economy, jobs and prestiege. So that the Nazis thought they were aryan.

Many noses and ears and breast of women were shorten and made to look smaller. As many eithnic groups had larger physical features.

There was once a Gypsy woman who was short and had only one huge breast. About fifty size. Gad had the breast amputated. And replaced the breasts with two large handsome nipples. Thats all! The fortyish Gypsy woman lost weight. Cut her hair short and you would think she was the all Aryan white fashion girl.

Many men also. They would pay a handsome price for the operations. Those that couldn' afford it. Would do security and work for the mother land. Like help out with helping the sick or transporting goods to the victims of the war in Germany.

Los Angeles Ca.
Fairfax district

Well! thank God! here we are. Riding in Bills custom made mercedes made the trip from Palm Springs to Los Angeles comfortable.

Now to find Dr. Gads house. I think he lives on this street if I am correct. Yes here it is. 617 Formosa street. Professor Cunningham stations his car right up the drive way. Dr. Gad does not drive anymore. He lives alone. Doctor Gads wife passed away a few years back. She was a pretty lady in her time. She was a professional seamtress. She also was a victim of the war in Hitlers Germany and made wonderdul clothes for the elites of that time. She also detected to England where she met Doctor Gad Rubens in her young twenty years.

Ah! lets get off young people and see what we can come up with. Knock! Knock! went into a humble home build back in the nineteen thirties. There were some modest shrubs around the house. Some flowers withering. Sarah and Omar streching their sore muscles and legs from the long one-hundred and twenty mile haul. The door opens and a hunch back squinty little wided eyed man with a long nose very tired looking about eighty years of age. Reacts and ask the strangers who they are.

Yes sir may I help you? Very professional the doctor asked? Well, Yes Gad! I am Bill! Bill Cunningham! Do you remember me? "Bill"? Well let me get my glasses. The voice sounds familar. Mr. Rubens voice very shaky and gentle. Yes! Gad You helped my mother and father escaped the nazis back in those days. I was a young man in my twentys.

Ok! "Bill." Oh yes. You are Sarahs and Gilberts boy. Yes! How you been? Its been some time. Nice to see you. "They both embrace". Come right in young people! May I get you something to drink. or some soup! I just made a whole pot of lentil soup. Gad grew up in Israel and worked with his father on a farm. This is where he learned to work with horses and later going to the university in Germany to become a veterinarian for horses. Thank you Gad! I want to introduce to you my daughter. This is Sarah! I named her after my mother. Sarah and Sabastian. "Bill' not revealing Omars real name at this moment. Omar, very quiet and observant.

Well nice to meet you young lady. Yes! and you do have your grandmothers eyes!" said' "Gad." How wonderful that you had children Bill. Maggie my wife was constantly ill from her hermones and we couldn't have a child. But thank god we had plenty of children to take care off all of our lifes.

Well! how sad Gad! would you perfer me to call you Gad or Mr. Rubens? Sarah asked respectfully.

Just call me Gad. This is good enough. Just don't call me horse lover! Ha, ha, ha Gad joked! for years this is all I heard from the Nazis and the goym! The goym being the gentils. Even as a child back home in Israel this is all I heard. Well don't you worry Gad! Gad it is! And this is my daughters friend Sabastian! Gad. Nice to meet you sir! Omar reached out and shook Gad s hand. Good looking boy Sabastian. "Gad", replyed". Well thank you sir.

Now have a seat. Bill suggested. Why sure Bill. "Gad," warmly replyed. And yourself too. Gad! let me check out the windows and doors. It is safe to speak I suppose. Why! we are in gods hands. Don't worry about a damn thing. Speak all you want. The floor is your! Thank you Gad.

Now Gad I don't know how close you have been following world events and this countrys moral and distination. Well somewhat I have been. Gad responded. Good listen Gad. You know the good lord says to fear no evil for he is with us! But he also told us to beware of the uncirumcised and infidels. I believe with all my heart that this country the leader of the free world has sold out to the devil. Gad I fear for our freedom. Yes I understand. I have been hearing this from different circles. There is nothing we can do! But hope to for best. And pray for the world to come to their senses. We have the same pattern happening that happen in Europe and Hitlers Germany. Many unemployed, High taxes, economic down trends and plagues and more plagues of disease and war. I have been through it all Bill. Its nothing new. That awful serpent. "Lucifer." Has gotton control of mankinds minds and spirits! You are so right! Gad! Yes and this bombing off the twin tower buildings. It was no accident! it was a damn man made conspiracy! Gad cryed out! What do they want! Another world war! Where millions of innocent lifes die?

Gad! I know this may sound insane. But the reason why we came here was for you to change our facial appearance and other body elements if you can. Ha,ha,ha. Well I can try. But I haven't practice in years Bill. Oh! daddy that would be dangerous! Sarah lashed out. Don't worry young lady. Don't be affraid but why change your appearance? You are very nice looking people.

Gad, aparently has not paid to much attention to the news recenty. Omars and Sarahs and doctor "Bill" William Cunningham photographs and profiles begun to appear on the F.B.I's most wanted list around the world. Bill had to be very careful not to expose to much of the real nature of his visit there. But If Mr. Rubens did find out that Bill and his family were hiding from the law. He wouldn't give a darn. Gad was a devoted human being. Devoted to the human conscious of the right to love your god and heritage.

Well Gad! We don't want to look normal. Or how should I say. We want a new look. More like the new age kids. You know like the punks on the sunset strip! Ha, ha, "Gad laughs". The reason is we have much wealth invested in banks. And we fear it will be taken away from us. We want to disquise our bodys and change our names also and become like rock stars. You know those kids that sing and dance rockin roll?

Humm now you really are up to something. Said Gad. Listen kids if you are hiding from something. "Gad called everyone under his age kids becouse he felt like he had seen it all." you don't have to worry about me sqealing. I have been there done that as they say. I can tell when you are exaggerating. Now why don't you start all over again Bill and tell me the whole story.

Oh! Gad. I am so sorry! I wasn't misinforming you. I was just going around and about so that you did not know what we really where up too! I did not want you to be involved in this matter. Well! Its my fault Gad! Sarah came out. No! Its my fault Gad! Revered Omar! My real name is Omar Bin Mohammud. I am not a terrorist! But I was a member. Assigned by an organization. I denounced moments before I learned I was to commit a world tragedy. A terrorist attack mission on the twin tower buildng here in America. I had nothiing to do with it sir Rubens! I met Sarah on the airplane headed Here for Los angeles and by gods mercy we fell in love with each other and Mr. Cunningham got us out past the airport authoritys by I adlibing to them. Telling them, I was a Mexican named Sabastian with a visa working for Miss Sarah as her manager of her cosmetic company.

Wow! This is more exciting than the nazi era. Mr. Rubens loved excitement. This has been his whole life. Up and down dare devil situations. Life was a mystery of bangs to him. Much like an Albert Einstein. He also detested war and the killing of innocent people.

Ok fine! I got the picture. Gad announced. Now let me see. Ok. You are going to need a place of refuge. I have a small bedroom in the back of my house here. By the way I believe you Omar. Thats a good name Omar. I believe your story. Though it isn't new. Many nazis in Hitlers Germany detected to the allies side. Thinking Hitler was wrong in his political war machine. And Hitler was a strong religious believer in God in his own fashion. I guess we can take religion and make it what we like.

Ok. Changing the subject. Surgery won't be nesessary. I worked for the movie studios. Of course Sarah ought to know of all the new modern cosmetic technologly there is! With out surgery.

All you will need a is a few mask and a bit of piercing some props. And you will be set. Oh thank god! I don't know what I would have done all cut up! Sarah cryed out. I should have known. But I guess the excitement dulls our Yes a bit gross, Omar suggested.

Well what do you say we get a goodnite sleep and in the morning we will figure out everything? Ok. Gad. It sounds great! Mr. Cunningham remarked. We are so thankful. Is there enough food here. If not we can maybe sneak out and get some. No! Gad responded with an uproar! You kidding! someone surly would reconized you. We have to stay low. I will get it some grocerys myself. Don't worry there is a grocery store right around the coroner from here.

I will go first thing tomorrow morning.

Ok fine Gad. But we would like to help with cash! Here is an advanced. Bill and Sarah pull out five, one-hundred dollar bills. Two from Sarah and three from Mr. Cunningham.

Oh! this is quite a lot! Smiled Gad. But I will take them. Ha,ha,ha.

Early the next morning Gad was off to the market. Mr. Cunningham was showering and Omar and Sarah were still sound of sleep. Sarah and Omar slepped in the same bed. To no ones surprise.

Good morning Dr. Rubens. The grocery store clerk welcomming Gad. Gad was the first customer in the store. It was 8 a.m. Goodmorning Jake. And what are we having this morning said Jake? Well I have company some relatives. How about some of your oatmeal and a couple gallons of sheep milk. Jakes boss imported sheeps milk from Israel. It was quite good. A little different from Americas Cow milk. But hey! It did the job.

Gad liked browsing around the store looking for specials. He was in a fix income. Like most senior citizens his age. Things were tough in America and there was talk about all out war with the terrorist groups and even any country that harbored terrorist. President George Fuller Jr. was the president and his administration was being tested to see what he might do to topple the economy and bring jobs back and stablize the worlds economys. There was world wide talk of a new world order.

Here you go Gad. Anything else? yes sir Jake. Here I have these other goodies. I have cash today. Good! "Replyed Jake." This helps me. Did you strike a gold mine "Gad?" Jake laughing. No. just got a little help from my relatives. Here you go a Franklin. Wow! don't know if I have any change so early in the morning let me go into the safe deposit box. I will be right back. Wondering around the back store room Jake gets the change and returns. Here we go! Your account is 45 dollars and 39 cents. And here is your change. Never seen you buy so much at a time Gad. Well thats life my boy! Now you have a very nice day. Same to you Gad! bye!

As Gad walked out the grocery store he saw the front page news of the Los angeles times. The headlines read. "TERRORIST SUSPECT IN LOS ANGELES". Back in Gads home Sarah and Omar had awaken. They were up and around. They had the television news channel on.

Wow! Look daddy! There we are! Theres a picture of us and Omar! We are really fugitives now! Don't let that worry you Sarah! They are wrong! Cryed out Mr. Cunningham. We are innocent. Omar is innocent. What are we going to do daddy? We are just going to be ourselfs. Play a little Russian rolet with the powers that be and see that we are justifyed in helping Omar and the couse for human rights. Said Bill.

Well goodmorning! Gad was pulling his little two wheeler basket with the gorcerys. Here I got some goodies. Here let me help you Mr. Rubens reached out Omar. Thank you son! Gad took a deep breath. You! should have seen the face on the clerk at the tore when I gave him the One-hundred dollar bill. His eyes popped out! Ha, ha, ha. Hope he didn't suspect something Gad. Mr. Cunningham scraching his head. Oh! No! Jake. He is a nice lad. He is very orthodox. And always minds his own business. But here. Look at the front page news of the Los angeles times! The picture of Omar and two small pictures of you Bill and Sarah proposing that you are harboring Omar! I was reading. Ah! nonsense! That will be the day when we harbor a Terrorist! Feeling uncomfortable was Bill. And in shock was Omar. Sarah was just cool.

Where can I hide my car Gad! I can't leave it out there in your driveway. Sure thing Bill. Just drive it by the side of the house to the back. And we can cover it with a tarp. Sounds good. In the mean time I will make breakfast said Gad. I will help you yawned Sarah. I will put the plates and drinking glasses in the table responded Omar.

Bill was fast putting his mercedes he had just bought two months before September 11,2001. On the back driveway of Gads house. He had it custom made. Inside the cd desk player he had a sliding plate where he kept thousands of fifty and one hundred dollar bills. At the most there was twenty-five thousand dollars there. He put it there for an emergency.

Back home in Pam Springs Bill was thinking how his friends, ex -friends now surly they all have turned against him after seeing his picture in the front page of the Los Angeles times. Accusing Bill of harboring a terrorist. Daddy! Breakfast is ready. Sarah whispering from out the window screen from the back of the house. Come and get your breakfast daddy. The house was in a lot. Like in the early nineteen hundred days of Hollywood. Ok dear I will be right in. Just checking some things here.

Bill looked around the house to see if any one was listening or suspecting anything. Not hardly. There were shrubs, dead flowers and tall cyprus trees as hedges with a tall wooden fence around. It was safe. But the "Fugitives", so called, Still had to keep a low profile.

Ok! here we are. Bill comming in from stationing his mercedes. What is for breakfast! Humm! I am so hungry this morning. Oatmeal, goats milk, pita bread, fruits, and lamb chops. Wow! what a meal! lets chow down. Yes and the tabled is served. responded Omar. This is just like back home in Egypt! Oh is this is were you from Omar? Answered Gad. Yes sir. I am from the poorer section of Cairo. The south side where they grow much corn. I was born there then later moved to the inner city. Great! With much enthusiasm responded Gad. Haven't been to Egypt in years. The last time I was there was when my father and a group of vets took a handful of lamed stallion horses back. We couldn't heal their injurys. So the rich sheik had us taken them back into Egypt and perform surgery there. In which we could not do! So the sheik had the horses slaughtered and dispersed the horse meal among poor. Ah! ah! How cruel! That is devilish to slaughter poor animals just becouse they are sick. I worked with greenpeace for some years and witnessed multitudes of dolfin and other animals in africa and even here in America. Killed for profit by poachers. And some were just killed for sport and left there to die. Justfied Sarah! This conversation is killing my appetite. Nosated Bill.

I am not to religious. But what do you say if we have a moment of silence. Then we begin to enjoy our delcious breakfast Gad? Fine with me. A little silence for the man or woman or what ever upstairs never hurt no one.

Back in Palm Springs at Lilys Mr. Bill Yacobs Cunninghams wife for many years was being bombared with the press. News reporters from all over the world were all over her house on pearl Drive. The great comedians Bob Hope's old house. There were television news men and magazines. You name it they were all there.

Even an ambulance came with the parmedics. It was reported that mrs. Lily Cunningham had fainted. Her sister that lived in San Francisco was on her way to be with her.

Mrs. Cunningham dear. Here take this pill. It will help you out. Whispered the nurse that was attending her. Well thank you nurse. Have they found that husband of mine? I am going to strangle him when ever I see him. How could he have done what he did. He never loved me so I never loved him either. We were married out of pure pleasure. I was richer than he. Well my parents left me a fortune. And he was a humble student going to the university. I helped him with his education and he became a great man. And got a damn! palestinian girl pregnant. Oh! My how sad! The nurse replied. What a bad thing. How did you feel? Well very bad of course. Oh! Oh! my back is hurting nurse. "Lily cryed out" Well here let me give you an injection. This well not hurt. Turn over. And I will administer it on you behind.

Mrs. Cunningham turns over. And while she is turning over she confesses that she had woman problems as a young lady that forbid her to have children.

Yes it wasn't Bills fault for going out on me. I encouraged him to have an affair with that Palestinian young girl. He wanted a child grown up in his old age. And he got one.

Lily's sister Mariam was at the doors steps of Lily's home. Getting off a taxi cab. Lily had called her the night before. Hoping she would know about Bills where abouts and disappearance.

Camera flashes started to go off! The crowd of reporters pulled their attention to the lady getting off the taxi cab. Please! Away from you! let me bye! Cryed out Mariam! What are you doing here! Who are you? And where is my sister? what have you done to her? "Are you Bill the terrorist ambassador's wife lady"? Shouted a reporter? I beg your pardon! Mariam, "Whacks", the reporter with her purse. How dare you speak of my brother in law this way!

What is your name lady? What are you to Ambassador William Cunningham? Never mind! Mariam lashed out! maid pecks out the window and advices her sister Lily that Mariam is at the door. Mrs. Cunningham Mariam is here my lady. The nurse relays the message to Lily. Well how wonderful your sister is here dear. Oh! open the door and let her in Mitilda! Before those crazy reporters kill her too! Mitilda opens the door in a hurry and lets Mariam in. One reporter bulls his way into the house and takes the picture of Lily and the inside off the house. Get the hell out off here! shouted Mariam! How dare you! The maid Mitilda and Mariam beat him with their shoes that they took off. These wackos! They haven't change since the old war days! They are the terrroist! The media is the couse of all the worlds ills! The door is slammed close. The reporters outside insist of their freedom of the press speech. By shouting "First amendment". Right. "FIRST AMENDMENT! "FIRST AMENDMENT"," FIRST AMENDMENT!

Back in the fairfax district in Los Angeles. "The fugitives" As every paper in the American nation called them. In the Arab nations and others they were heralding them as heros. In Iran, Iraq, Afganastan, South Africa, Egypt and so Bill, Sarah, Omar and Dr. Gad Rubens had finished their breakfast and were gluded to the television. They couldn't believe the horror and evil gossep they were saying about them. They were innocent and so was Omar alias Sabastian. Now Dr. Gad Rubens was involved.

Television News station WWN had a special report on the life Sarah and Omar. The anchor reporter was reporting that Sarah was the all American girl. How could such a successful thirty year old of age who had her own in cosmetics and the world in her hand run off with a would be terrorist! Sarah was the model girl of any free nation on earth. They reported her failed marriages and interviewed her ex-husbands. One called her a low down nasty sneaky 'Bastered". These were the exact words! Harry. Her first marriage husband. When she was twenty-one. Was one sour cookie. Having been in the then Persian Gulf war in kuwait Arabia when president fourty-one the old George Fuller Sr. was president. The war, Did a great deal of brain damage to his brain. Many of Americas young soldiers were believed poisoned with germ warfare. Chemicals that couse great immune defenciency damaged to the brain, body. Then 'death", as the ultimate. These germ warfare was considered the third world countrys only real defense along with terror on the street suicide bombing agains the rich powerful cyberspace and star war western nations as they called themselfs.

Sarah, Omar and the two senior gentlemen were not very touched by such lies the press was reporting. It was time to come to their senses.

What can we do Bill? Gad cryed out! We are surrounded. Gad had begun to crack up. Maybe its wrong what we are doing? No! Gad don't worry! I have a plan. We must never give our selfs up.

"Said Bill. "Maybe we should give our selfs up! "Omar resumed". It isn't right that you go to prison becouse of me. Its all my fault! I will give my self up now! No! don't be foolish! Omar! I know this world to damn! well! We will get no justice! No! No one will believe our story. We would be fools giving ourselfs up! You are talking the death penalty for you Omar! and Life in prison for us for harboring you! I am not going to prison in my old age. And Gad cannot afford this either.

And I want to anounce that Omar and I are going to have a baby! Sarah mouthed out! What! "Mumbled Bill." Honey! How can this be! We have no time for this! Yes daddy you are going to be a grand daddy! Praise the lord! Laughed out loud Gad! This calls for a celebration and not panic! Let me bring out my best Sabbath wine and kosher food! Every one make yourself a home and relax. Stay a while. Turn off that stupid t.v. and let me prepare a nice dinner for tonite. And play some nice kosher music. You are so right! Gad. Here let me help you. Leeping with joy was Bill. "Well thank you Gad for understanding". Sarah dropping all her stress and tention. Omar hid in a embarassed. Don't be embarassed Omar! Gad singeled Omar out. This child that is in Sarahs womb! well be a blessing to us all. Maybe the savior!

Back in Palm Springs on pearl street. Lily and Mariam her sister were sobbing like chlidren. The nurse was trying to calm them both. Giving them sedatives to keep them calm.

Sister," cryed Lily." How could this have happen? This is a nightmare. What had gotten into the mind of Bill? He never took drugs or drank. He wasn't religious or anything. I don't know sister. You now how the devil is going around foolin everyone. Well I thought you and Bill where so in love Lily. You told me he couldn't live with out you. I lied! I just damn lied! we haven't sleped in the same bed since he had that crazy girl bastard daughter of his. "Sarah". Oh! she is a nice young girl scoffed Mariam. She is so sweet. She just appears that way. Rebuked Lily! She is one of the nastiest little swine I have ever had to raise in my life! Lily! Scorned Mariam! Speak nice of your adoped daughter. She is not my daughter! Mariam! God forbid. That damn husband of mine. Ex- husband couse I don't want anything to do with him ever again. Ever since he got that Palestina girl pregnant.

Mariam never knew the real story behind Bill and Lilys relationship. She did not know that Lily had ask Bill to have an affair with the young Palestian girl seventeen years his minor. Mariam did know her sister was barren. But it never crossed her mind that Bill with such high standards of living could have had an affair with another woman becouse of her sisters extreemly arrogant attitude.

CHAPTER 7

ONE TEAR GOD, TRILLIONS FOR AMERICA

Bill was wondering and thinking of a plan to perserve his familys intergrity. With out anyone in his family or his fellow countrymen being hurt So he suggest something out of the blue and courages. While Sarah, Omar and Gad were having a wonderful time feasting. Omar was so over excited he was having a son or daughter and Sarah in her early year "thirty", Was jassed to the max. Her moon cycle did not come as it was the time and this was the notice she believed that she had sibling on the way.

Well. People! lets try something exciting. We are innocent aren't we? Why yes! They all responded in a shout! Then why are we hiding? Aren't we free and have our god given rights? What do you say we go to a large park here in Los Angeles and have a picnic and celebrate my grandson's to be." welcome birth"!

Oh! daddy, No! Oh! No sir! exclaimed Sarah, and Omar! We will be risking our lives! Gad remained silent.

Now come on! kids! What are we afraid off? We have money don't we? I don't care if I lose all my lifes hard savings money defending my family and now especially my grandson to be born. I will pour my every last dime for my grandson! If we have to fight our case in courts all over the world for the rest of our lifes. I don't care. We are innocent! And my grandson is not going to run around like a fugitive at large!

So what do you say we go for it? Huh?

Your father is right kids! Gad said out loud. The best way to solve problems is to look them right in the face. we have nothing to hide. Omar what do you think? "Sarah, retreated". Omar quiet and shy. Was in a far away thoughts. His dark Egyptian big eyes wide open. I don't know Mr. Cunningham. I am so afraid. Its me they are really after and not you. Look here my son! Bill extreemly angered. It is my Blood they are after! And you son and you daughter, And now this, "Touching Sarahs womb", Is my youngest child. In which I will die for!

As Gad was preparing to exit his house to water his plants outside. Neighbors on his street were running in panic to get into their homes. Mr. Rubens stay inside your house! They have bombed New York city again and the town is on fire. wat? Exclaimed Gad in his jewish accent. Yes some one fired a missile and all of New York city came tumbling down a Jewish cryed out! Oh! my god! What is it! Bill came running out why all the commotion? Bill turn on the news. New York city has been bombed again. "Gad very nervous." Sarah and Omar turned on the television news. Every channel was tuned in to the most nightmarish tragedy in American history. Some desperate society that hated the United States of America had attacked the red white and blue to boot. Their was the axis of evil powers Iran, Iraq, and North korea. Who had every weapon of mass destruction at their desposal. Then their was China who had become the riches nation on earth. And the most populated with one and one half billion people strong. They had a two hundred million man army that was at anytime going to unleash their forces on the western nations. China was believed to be the mother land of the axis of evil powers. The country of Russia who was one half in Asia and the other half in Europe. Could go either way. They were a free nation these days and worked along the Nations Alliance Treaty Organization or N.A.T.O. An organization composed of the most powerful western free nations that were none communist. Who could have attacked America? It was November almost two months after the twin tower bombings. Was it the Al- Qaida? The axis of evil powers Or some conspiracy within the American government that had sold out to form a new goverment within the borders of the United States of America? As some believed.

Bill was excelerated! Now I remember! All those years I was an Ambassador I never took all those meetings seriously. I went with the joints chiefs of staff and the president to all those meetings to brief us on the future of America. I could never understand what they were really talking about. They spoke of a day of armagadon. And a brand new American prosperty. They also gave me documents of a whole new American order. The United States of America was to become the model state of a world order.

What are you speaking about daddy?

proclaimed Sarah. Yes don't you see. Oh! my god! We have to get out of this country! We need to go back to Israel! We can be safe their. Cryed out loud." Bill". We are doom if we stay here.

You are right Bill. "Gad answered." Hitler did the same thing to Germany to put in his "Third Reich".

I have heard of this happening to America.

Yes and even I have heard of this with the Al-Qaida remarked Omar. Their were rumors that the American heirchy wanted to put a muslim powered goverment to replace the christian philosophy here. But we all knew this was a propaganda. And the Al-qaida took advantage of the situation to committ terrorist acts.

Wow! this is frighting. A confused Sarah lashed out. I have heard for years that there are camps and ready made tent citys for a disaster.

Look! The president is comming on to give a speech! Lets hear what he has to say!

"Dear Americans". George Fuller jr. speaking to the nation in a undisclosed safe area from the Bombings in New York city.

"Our nation has been attacked by Unlawful enemy forces. We will use all our god given resources to rid these cowards who have killed scores of innocent lifes in the heart of New York city. There will be other attacks that follow soon. We urge all Americans to stay calm and lowly. All borders will be closed from in comming and out going travel. We must put all are borders states and citys under Marshall law and alert. We have invited our allies of Europe and all free nations to to work with us. Please coraporate with them as it is for our own security and interest.

We pray to god to over come our enemys that will soon be put under. May god bliss America and the people of this great nation."

In the mean time Bill's leg was hurting. He had lost his cane and tryed to quit smoking his cuban cigars. What are you doing daddy? "singled out Sarah". You did'nt even listen to the presidents speech. Yes I did my dear. Och! My leg is hurting. I lost my cane and have been walking with out it. Yes I have notice daddy. Maybe you better sit down. Yes here Bill. Compassion was given from "Gad". Sit here on this soft chair. We don't have time Gad. I am using your phone and trying to call a French airline pilot friend of mine for many years. He owns a few a airplanes. Maybe we can hitch a ride to France then Israel on his planes. We can be safe and have immunity there. But we need to get out of here fast. All airports will be closed. But we can disquise our looks and pass as French rock stars tourist going home. We can get fake pass ports.

Wow! that will be hard to do! Cryed Omar. Nothing is impassable my boy! Replied Bill.

Yes! Henri! How are you? This is Bill Cunningham! How are you big guy? Yes I am fine. No! 1 am not a fugitive. It's all a big mistake. We did not kill or rob anyone. Yes, I do have a problem. This is why I am calling you. But I am afraid you don't trust me any more.

henri Mendes was a young, Well almost young French pilot that fought in the Vietnam war. He was about fifty-eight years of age. His father a well to do French business man that owned wine plantations across Europe. Had left Henri his wine business in which Henri converted it into a fleet of airliners. He called, "Napoleons Warriors". He had six beautiful sky ships that made him a fortune at a reasonable rate.

"I will tell you what Bill". Yes I know all airports are grounded till further notice. I can't see any sky ship getting off the ground for days till these attacks are controled. I got a call from the aviation department. And ordered my company to ground my ships or they would be consfiscated.

Oh! Henri! Well! I will tell you what. I really want to thank you from the bottom of my heart. But please not a word to any one that we spoke on the phone. Please trust me. I am innocent and so is my family. I wanted to hitch a ride to France then to a safe place from there.

Just then Sarah yanks the phone away from Mr. Cunningham and has a conversation with Henri. Sarah! what are you doing dear! Hello! Hello! Hello!

Yes sir! I am Sarah Cunningham. Bill's Daughter. Whats that? Yes Sarah! I am sorry I am yelling sir. But we have an emergency to run. We have little time. Whats that? I am in my thirtys sir. I want to ask you. How much will you sell one of those 747's to me for? Yes I can afford it. Better yet I will give in exchange my cosmetic company for one of your 747's.How much am I worth? Fifty million dollars. Lock, stock and barrel. How can you know? Sarah! Thats to much money to give away dear. Said Bill. Yes Sarah! lashed out Gad.

Ok! You know how to use the internet? Go to www dot Sarahcunn dot com and you will find my business records and magazine articles about my life and financial holdings. It gives the name of my bank and how much I am worth. How can you make the exchange wth me? I will use a code and sign everything over to you. You can get arrested for dealing with a felon? Look sir I am not a felon. Don't ever call me that again! understand! Be nice Sarah! Bill cryed out. And who can fly the sky bird?" I can screamed out Omar". I took flying lessons when I was in Florida. My boyfriend can sir. Sarah tired of answering his questions. Well you want fifty big ones or not! I don't need you! I can go some else place. Sarah was showing her expertice in business dealings. She could be very shrewd. Ok! listen very carefully Henri. Thats your name right? Yes listen. I will call you. don't call me. Do you have caller I. d.? Ok good. In about one- half hour I will call you. daddy has you number. And by that time you should know who I am financially.

Now! I want you to go to the airport and fill up one of those big birds with all the petroit needs. Enough to fly us across the Atlantic ocean and to France. If the police at the airport ask you what you are doing. Tell them you are just maintencing your planes. In case the marshall law is raised. Sneak plenty of food and water and beverages and toilet paper. Ok? Yes. Now when we make a run for the plane at the airport. Please have it running. We will take care of the rest.

I will leave my financial code card number in your computer email adress. You must trust me please! In my I.D. card I have a "Will" that reads like this." As for any reason if I should die or my person should be missing for up to one year. Then This code card number will go to the person that holds it in their person." Do you understand me? Yes sir. I will call in a half hour. Leave me your e-mail address and business will be done.

What is that? What if the F.B.I. has already infiltrated my code name? They can't. I took care of that years ago. Just trust me Henri. When you call me in a half-hour I will have more details as to were we will meet. Ok? Ok later! and thank you Henri sweety.

Oh thank god for that man! Omar raising his head. Who is he? And how are we going to do this operation?

Well I am not going any where sqeaked out Gad. I have had enough of running all of my life. I will stay here and pray for you. I will face my distiny with grace. I am not afraid of anything anymore. Oh! Gad! We meant to take you with us. "Said Bill". Ha, ha, ha, forget it. You think I am going to run and make a break for the airport at my age? Ha, ha, ha. Well we are going to compensate you Gad! Sarah speaking in a firm voice. Only two-thirds of my money is in my savings under a different name not Sarah. But one-third is in a bank in Switzerland under another name not Sarah, Gad. The name is, "Bill". Yes there is eighteen million dollars in that safe. Its all your Gad, and this is the code along with the name "Bill."

Sarah showing Gad the code while Bill and Omar stand by the side in awed. Wow! You really are a beautiful person Sarah! Omar standing with tears running down his eyes.

Sarah! Gad whispering with a shaky voice. What are you doing? This is not nesessary dear. Oh! you don't have to do this. This is your hard working money dear. Save it so when you get to Israel. Is only money Gad. There is much more where this comes from. Don't worry.

Bill by now was in twilight zone. Sarah was in full charge of the mission. Bill had no money to give. His "will" went all to Lily and charities.

All he had in cash was the twent-five thousand in his car that he had already forgotten he had. Because of all the commotion. But then remembered. Gad! Here are my keys to my mercedes. you have it when we leave. And If you look in the cd department. Thats were we play music. I have reward for you. But don't go there till after we leave. Humm! Ok responded Gad. And Gad never questioned the reward.

Well, now lets get to work. What a wonderful life this is. The cost of freedom. We shall over come said a black leader once. "Words of wisdom from Sarah". Gad, Take out your cosmetic kit. And begin to disquise us. I will start cutting my hair short and then coloring my hair black.

What do you suggest this over grown bear shold look like Sarah? "Bill" suggested. You daddy can color your hair black also. "Bills hair was pure white. And you Omar can color your hair blond. Blond? Wow! I always thought what I would look like with blond hair. But I don't have white skin! Don't worry, Gad squeaked out. White is only skin deep." Ha, ha, ha. They all laughed.

Ok. I have a plan for us all." Sarah beginning to use more control as she gave her worlds life fortune to save her family. "When I go call Henri in exactly twenty-five minutes. I am going to suggest to him we dress up as his maintainance mechanics. So that when we make a run for the airport and the plane. The police that are guarding the airport will think we are part of his crew.

Ha, ha, ha. That is a very clever idea Sarah. Yes I saw this in movie. Only in the movies cryed out loud Gad. So! Lets get our plan straight so that nothing goes wrong. We can't afford any mistakes said Omar. We have come to far for foolishness.

Sarah had cut her hair short like a French fashion girl. Her eye brows and lashes were a dark black she had put on with mascara and eye pencil. Her eye lids were colored an off blue. And the most noticeable was her dark red lips. She looked so hot and nasty you thought she was a call girl.

Honey! Proclaimed Bill. You are way off! take some of your coloring off or soften it up a bit. You are advertising to much. Yes Sarah. Omar also concerned. Ok. I will soften the mascara and lipstick. In the mean time Omar was dying his hair blond. Gad had also prepared a face mask that would give Omar softer features. Although Omar was a very good looking Egyptian boy. Bill was also coloring his hair dark.

Around the world in other news. Another missile had hit in the heart of America. The free nations were in a all out alert. England who was the United States close's ally was also being bombed. All of Europe was paralized and living in fear. China and the so called rogue nations where defing United Nations orders to stop the terror. They denied that they were the problem. They blamed it all on the Al-Quida and other terror organnizations. In Palestine. Israel and the libians and syrians and palestians were at war by now. Scores had lost their lives. The Russians were staying quiet. But how long before they came into the scene of war was the centurys question. They were the most powerful weapons of mass destruction on earth. Next to America of course. The Russian mafia and K.G.B. had bought almost all of the American banks. And were pretty solid financially.

The chinese had infilterated all of South America and owned most of the banks there. They had great military prowness like never before seen. The Chinese had a two-hundred million man army ready to travel across the worlds oceans to conquor The Americas.

Sarah was looking cookie as she went out of Gads home unnotice by the people on the street. If they did notice her. They probably thought she was a punker from sunset boulivard. There were many in these days as in many from the past years. Young kids that liked the fads and fashions of dressing with black leather pants, skirts, and long black leather boots up to there knees. Many colored their hair, different colors like red orange, purple, lilac, dark black and other colors.

These pukers as some called them. Could be very discussting. Sarah was only going to be a punker for a short time before her real life turned back to normal she thought.

Yes sir hello? Sarah had found a pay phone in the corner of a street next to a little grocery store where Gad went shopping. Yes sir! Henri? I am Sarah. The half-hour is up. Did you read my website? Yes? No! I haven't e-mailed you my code number yet. I have a better plan for us. Yes? You do too? Tell me yours first then I will tell you mine. Okay. Oh! You will pick us up at our location? Humm. Ok! In the eveing? Ok. Thats exactly what I told my family. Yes to dress up like the mechanics from your work crew. Yes. You plan to be the pilot! and take us to Israel!

Holy! Moses! That sounds wonderful! I love you! Henri! Then I can give you your recompensation in person! Ha!, ha, ha. Yes here is my location. Pick us up on the corner of fairfax and beverly boulivard. Ok? Ok! dear. Bring the work clothes. Yes we will be here about an hour after the sun goes down. That would be around sevenish p.m. You have someone there already filling up the plane with gas!. Great! So that when we get there to the airport all we have to do is board and we are ready to go airborn. Great! good plan Henri! See you in about three hours. Hum bye, bye.

Hi guys! Sarah walking into the door of Gads house after knocking and getting the clear from Mr. Cunningham to walk in. Hello dear. What did you plan out? Daddy We have a very good plan. Henri is going to pilot his airplane for us. He thought it would be better. Great! I told you he was a smart and swell cookie. He's a honest Frenchman. "Reasured Bill" Well either that or he is just afraid his airplane's will be taken away from him if the police find out he had some dealings with harboring us.

Omar went into seclution into one of Gads rooms and kneeled by a bed side to pray. Gad was starting to feel the pinch of missing the gang when they would leave. "I am really going to miss you young people. I wish I could something more to keep you here. "Gad said." You have done more than enough my friend responded Bill. We are so grateful to you! Yes Gad. You are good people. And thank you so much for taking us in.

Omar! where our you? Omar came out off Gads den smiling. Here I am. I was doing some chatting with my soul. That is good for the spirit Gad praised. I am most grateful Mr. Rubens for taking me in. "If it wasn't for me," Bill and Sarah wouldn't be in this mess. No! You are wrong Omar! it is all my fault. I was the one who flirted with Omar in the airplane back from the state of Texas. And I was the one who made the moves for Omar to come with me and live with me. Now I am with child. And I love it. Cryed out Sarah. Ha, ha, ha. Oh! How beautiful it must be to feel little one. Huh? Mommie? "Gad responding to Sarahs remarks." Sure does! They all get a laugh and hug each other and say their last goodbyes with tears in their eyes. Sarah Bill and Omar had about an hour an a half before going the street to meet Henri. In the mean time they had some soup as the last supper.

The scenario was set. Bill, Sarah and Omar had left Gad Rubens the horse surgeon and good friend for the trip of their lifes. They did not have the slightest idea what the future held. Bill Cunningham might have expected this. He had been around and seen much in is life. Also experience quite a bit. Those times in Hitlers Germany was the ultimate to him. Things couldn't get any worst. Sarah was the baby of the bunch. This was actually her first real experince and tribulation of her life. She saw it as an adventure.

As they left Gad Rubens home they walked up to the corner of the main street that led to the main freeway. The street was fairfax and beverly boulivard. There was a phone there and a little grocery store. As Sarah and the felons were waiting around looking like street punks from a hollween movie. Bill asked that they seperate some distance so that they did not look conspicious. On the street there were also young kids hanging around. Smoking cigarrets trying to be cool. It must have been their hang out.

Oh! daddy! I forgot to ask Henri what kind of vehicle he was driving up in. Well its to late now. I hope he has a good imagination as to distinguish. He knows that I am big fellow. Let me go into the store and get a snickers chocolate bar.

said Sarah. Omar was wondering around kind of nervous with a head of blond hair looking like Paul Mc Carney with brown skin. "Omar" Relax! Cryed out Bill. We'll be out of here soon.

Honk! Honk! Went a mini, dark green shiny van driving up the curb. Sarah dear lets roll cryed out Bill. Henri is here dear! Omar, suspicious checking out the van as to see who it was and who was driving it. Out ran Sarah and breathed a sign of relieve. Ok cool is he here? Yes dear this is him. I reconized his face.

The mini's van front window opened. Bill is that you?

Yes! this is me! Henri! How are you? Excited was Bill. Here kids hurry up nd get in the van. Sarah and Omar wasted no time to jump in the back seat and acamodate themselfs. The van was fairly new and had a nice fresh odor like it just been taken from the factory.

Well here I am in too said Bill. Lets get this baby going. So! how in the hell have you been Henri? It has been some time. Here put on your safty seat belts or we well be pulled over said Henri. We are all tied up resumed Sarah. So! were's my money giggled Henri. Relating to Sarahs big give away pay to Henri for sneaking her and her family out of the country. It will be given you onced we are almost to our distination. Ha, ha, ha. Sorry but you didn't think I was that easy. Did you? Ha, ha, ha. Henri laughed.

No! being Bills daughter. I imagined some resemblense. Ha, ha, ha. That's ok. I trust your good name.

As Henri was driving west towards the pacific beach cities. He had to make a left turn by a major hiway. There were many American soldiers stopping traffic. They had a check point.

Oh! Just relax gang! Henri whispered. Remember you are part of my crew that maintance my fleet of airplanes. Try not to speak if you don't have too. If the check point soldier ask you where are we going. Just answer to the airport shop.

We'll do Mr. Henri. Replyed Sarah. Oh! And in the back of your seat there are your overalls. Put them on! You are going to need them. They are easy to slip on. Humm, The mechanic clothe. Cool! They look very sexy charmed Sarah. Here lets put them on!

The soldiers at the check point had blue helmets. They were of the united nations international peace keeping police force. Henri being a airplane owner and pilot knew them to well. There wasn't a flight that he wasn't confronted with them.

Good eveing sir. Said the uniformed officer. Good eveing sir. Replied Henri in his cute French accent. Henri was from south France. He thought he was of Basque orgin. Which they don't consider themselfs French per say. And where are we going to this eving? Proclaimed the officer. I am going to the airport. I am the owner of a French based airline business. Whats it called? Replied the officer. Its called "Basque Muru" International airlines. The soldier was a French native and reconized the airline name. Oh! you are the owner? Yes said Henri. Here is my license and papers to prove it.

Well anyone who is a country man is a friend of mine. is these your crew? The French officer resided in a broken english accent. Looking at Bill and Sarah and Omar. Yes they work for me. We are doing some maintance today. Ok, bon! fantastique! A bit of French Good! Fantastic! You may move on! "Cho". or goodbye. Said the country man offical. Henri moved on fast out of the checking point lane. He did not want to start a country mans conversation there. Knowing that Frenchmen loved to chat and there was no stopping them.

The checking point was packed with in comming traffic. To the point where people got out of there cars to strech out there legs. Henri and the gang were very lucky to have had a fast lane and make it out on time for the journey of their lifes.

Well, that was an experince Omar whispered in a loud voice. Yes it was said Bill. Now all we have is a fifhteen minute ride to the airport and bombs away said Sarah. Yes indeed replyed Henri.

As Henri turned on the van radio to listen to the news. The reporter on the news was warning the Los Angeles citizens about a possible missile attack in the Los Angeles area. We interupt this program to bring you the latest news on a possible terrorist attack in the Los Angeles area. 'Said the reporter." We just got word that a missile lunched by "China" Could be on its way no later than ten minutes from now. The United States government has taken measure to intercept the missile as soon as possible. Please we urge all Angelinians to stay calm and quiet and protect your self much as you can.

Wow! Hold on gang! I am stepping on the gas. Hold on! I will radio ahead to my crew that I have there to have the plane ready to go airborn!

Hello! Henri using his van radio transmitter! Yes come in! Jacque! come in! Yes this is Jacque! Jacque! This is Henri! Is the bird all gased up? Yes it is boss! Jacque said in the other end. Ok! keep the plane running and drive it on the runway close the doors for now and when you get to the runway twelve. Slep the doors back down again. I will catch up with you with my van and board the plane. I have some company comming with me. Ok Boss! You sound excited! Is something the matter. Replyed Jacques with much conceren. Everything is fine Jacque! Have all the crew get on Board and prepare to fly out in the blue! We are in operation "Blue Bird".

Operation "Blue Bird" was the ulitmate in a crisis. A code way of saying it was a matter of life or death situation. You got it boss! Welcome on board! Jacques Reinstated his composure. Alarming himself to be calm and cool.

There was no turning back. For the fugitives that were at large. Their lifes where at stake. There was no turning back. It was to Israel and the land of the holy. The middle east was in shambles. But Israyal and Egypt became good friends. And these two nations were the only havens for the people of the book. Egyptians like Isralites and christians could find a haven and ammesty if they were being persecuted or being accused of some crime. From around the world.

Full speed ahead said Henri. We have exactly ten minutes to barge right through the hiway and onto the heavens ally.

Henri was speeding as fast as his van could move. He was passing cars and big heavy traffic right and left. Some police patrolmen spotted him and let him speed. While others begun to chase him with their red lights on.

We have a runaway dark green van. Year, seems modern, radioed one hiway patrolman. It is going south east on the Santa Monica freeway. Can we get some back ups? Well do said the lady dispacher at the pacific beach station.

Hold on gang! We have lived like champions and we shall be caught like champions.

Thats if we get caught. Remember you have millions of dollars at stake. And an unborn child on the way and are giving our lifes for. Yes! Screamed Omar! I am the father! And I am the grandfather Henri! So! don't wreck my boy! Cryed out Bill.

Oh! my love. Then we better hurry in a safe way. Lashed out Henri.

Henri radio'd the crew at the airport to have medical assitance ready just in case. And he cautioned that they had a pregnant woman on board.

Yes Jacque! Prepare all medical supplies. In case of miscarrage. Exclaimed Henri to Jaques. Sarah started to get nervous and goose pimples as Omar. She will be find cautioned Bill. She is a big girl. Omar moved over to Sarah and put his arms around her. He kisses her.

I don't mean to be rude or to scare you but we must be prepared for all things. I want to caution you now that we are making a fast run for the airplane. I am not stopping at the gates and check point to get the ok to pass through. We are going directly to the airplane and are going to have to hurry. Get out of the van and run onto the boarding ramp stairway into the plane. We might not have anytime at all for anything but board till the big bird is in the sky. Yes this is just like in the movies except we are the good guys!

Okay hold on! We are here at the airport we are ramming right through the blockade dividers.

Crash! Went the sound as Henri boomed right through the blockade dividers made of wood and cement. One of The vans sides was dinted but the gang was alright. Dozens of police cars and patrolmen were following behind. Other patrolmen were warned ahead at the airport to be ready for the green van that was driving suspiciously and wrecklessly into the airport. Stop! Stop! An arm guard warned! Henri did not stop and kept going seventy miles an hour on a fifteen mile zone. Runway twelve was just six-hundred feet away. And the big concorde French "Basque Muru", Was insight waiting full speed ahead.

Finally as Henri approached the big megaton light blue concorde with the large company letters "Basque Muru airlines" written across the body of the plane. And a colored drawing of a beautiful tanned bikini woman on the body of the plane. He hurried the gang to get off the van and run up the ramp stairway.

Hurry! Hurry! Waiting for nothing. As the van coasted in braking and burning tire. The tires of the van smeared the concrete by the runway with a dark and smelly odor. A big smokey cloud of smoke could be seen not only from Henri's van but from the police cars who apparently never changed their oil from their patrol cars.

Hurry get out! And run upside the plane. Sarah, Omar and Bill did just that. They wasted no time. In fact they beat Henri up the ramp stairway onto the big bird. Leaving the doors on the van wide open. And even Bill did not need a cane or cigar to make him activate. The cops were about six hundred feet behind.

Henri ran into the cock pit as he was the head pilot. As Jacques was the co-pilot that was preparing the take off. Fine every one inside? Press switch to close doors! Full speed ahead! Snap on your safty belts. This big bird is off!

The concorde believed to have been build in France and England was the worlds fastest and most luxuriest airliner. It could carry as much as one-hundred passengers from New York city to London England in just three and one half hours. The take off speed was as much as two-hundred and fifty miles an hour. And it was rated a "Mach Two" or it could fly twice the speed of sound!

Ok! We are off! Bye! Bye! cruel! world! Laughed Henri. Bon voyage.

The airliner was taking off slowly up the runway twelve. Taking direction the wheels moving slowly then faster and faster then the big light blue bird. Sprung her wings and a big gush of power and boom of air lifted the concorde onto the dark blue skys. Like if it was the "Big Bang" and the biginning of the creation of the world.

Bang! The sound of lighting and lighting illuminated the dark blue sky. In just a few good minutes the big bird was already in San Diego county territory. The cops were all gathered below in frustration. About two dozen police cars and military patrolmen. They did not want to fire their weapons becouse it would not do them any good. The concorde was way out of sight by now and was bullet proof.

The airport security avation dispach officer called on the military units to take over the runaway airliner.

Hello! Yes! This is airport dispach at L.A. X. Please come in air force base. Yes! this is air force base! Yes sir. We have a runaway concorde airliner headed do south with suspects running from the law. Can you send some F-14 fighters to check them out. You might have to force the concorde to return and land back here at the airport. The passengers were illuting the police on a small mini van. Yes. Said the other voice at the end of the other side. We have satilites and just spotted an image on the dark skys. We have fighters on their tails. Over and out. Thank you for the alert. The other voice on the other side which was from homeland security base near San Diego California was monitoring all flights. And Henri's big bird "The Basque muru". Was about to be visited by four F-14 fighters. Ha, ha, ha went Henri. Nothing like flying in the night. You can see all the stars, Is everyone alright? Henri adressed the crew and Omar Bill and Sarah. Henri was looking through his t.v. monitor. Yes we are fine! The crowd belted on their seats. When do we have dinner! Sarah yelled out! Ha!, ha laughed Henri. Wait till we get across the Mexican border. We have a few moments to cross then we chow down.

Ok! fine, But I need to go potty. Squirmed Sarah. Sorry but we are not high enough in the sky for you to get up. Please hold on till we hit a few more altitude feet. Yes we have to go too! Cryed out Bill and Omar.

Mexico was only a few miles to the border. Much of the drug trafficking that came across from South America was legal now. And the illegal immigration was an open border. There was free trade on all levels. All of the Americas from Canada to the tip of Argentina was one big hiway to the sky. Most of the third world country's had cought up with the U.S.A. And the terrorist bombings of the twin tower buildings was the beginning of the end for the red white and blue.

Oh! my god! I just heard on the radio that Los Angeles has been destroyed almost completely by enemy missiles! Cryed out Henri! Oh! my god! every one on the concorde sat there very quietly.

Please crew prepare for the worst. There are heavy dark clouds up ahead. Just when Henri was announcing this there was a harsh voice that came on the concordes speakers. "Please stay calm and direct the aircraft onto the Mexico city airport". Please abide by our orders or we will have to shoot you down. Said the harsh voice from a f-14 jet fighter flying along side the concorde.

Oh! My! Yelled Henri. Now how do I know where Mexico city is? We got a doggie on our tails. Ha, ha, ha. Watch me make him disappear. Henri blew some kind of smoke from his exust pipes and from the side of his wings. His plane must have been custom made couse he had all kinds of tricks up his concordes sleeves.

Henri eased on his speed of the plane and made a jet fighter dive look like childs play and boom the giant concorde dropped down some wild feet across the foggy wicked dark universe. Sarah was tide up and had her seat belt fasten while sitting down on the toilet taking a pee. Woe! Sarah went. What is happening! Bill, Omar and the crew were sucked to their seats by the turbulance. The concorde was fast diving in the thick black clouds. The f-14's jet fighters had disappeared in the night fog and were no where to be seen.

Henri cryed out. God! help us! I"ve lost control of the airplane! We are going to crash! Oh! My God!

YEAR 2050 A.D.

It was a sunny blue skys day on the white sandy beach with surf in the year 2050. When Sarah, Omar, Bill and some of the crew about three. That their dead like bodys were washed onto the coast line. There was some bit of greenery along the beach. But not a living human being or bird or animal to be found. There was a space station like structure inland. There were people but not of total human form.

Look boss a voice in the wilderness by the space station called out. There are objects floating to shore on the east beach. The voice was not human. It was like mechanical. Yes I see it. Thank you. Take a crew and see what we have there.

Skinny was a intergalactic cosmic Sapian. Who was half human and half intergalatic cosmic.

Wow! what is this? One would think. An intergalactic cosmic sapian are human beings taken from planet earth to represent the new cosmic order that went beyond the new world human order as preplaned by the ruling elites of the late planet earth that was onced ruled by America and her allies. That world died and perished in a great world war that killed everything in site. These cosmic intergalactic sapians who have some human genetics were very carefully diciphered and taken out before the destruction of the earth. And were procreated by the cosmic intergalactic order. Skinny and his boss "Axis of Good" or better known as Axis were born into the intergalactic time zone.

Skinny and the crew of a couple of his cosmic kind went down to the beach to check out the objects that were washed onto the sandy shore. The shore was only feet away.

Gee! Said Skinny. My transmitter reciever is imaging human bodys. Axis like all cosmic sapians had little tiny cone like papilla's on top of their head. The cosmic sapians did have human flesh as human's did in the old world. Nor did they have any type of old world earthly flesh. But had a leathery type of body. Their heads were round and had no eyes. Their papilla was their reciever and connection to their brain function. They were tall. About seven feet with long legs and skinny bodys with no hands just long arms. Each of the cosmic sapians were different colors of bodys. Axis was the color of the blue sky. Becouse he was the chief cosmic sapian. Skinny was a light red orange. The other two cosmic sapians were green ad yellow. Each color representing the light of the order of the rainbow.

Hi there boss. As skinny addressed Axis. Yes Skinny come in. These objects are humans. From the old world. I reconized their eyes. Cryed out Skinny. Oh! My. I will walk over to inspect them myself. "Cheered" Axis.

As Axis was walking half way to the humans that were washed onto the shore. His papilla reciever on top of his head began to act up. Knocking Axis to the ground. Yeak! yike!! Ouch!!!!! Electrified out Axis. Axis was knocked out for a moment and began to see his whole life before him. He began to see his true orgins when he was being concieve and when he was being born. Way back on the old earth time zone. One of the bodys had some form of radiation that was cousing Axis recievers to detonate.

I am receiving signals of a human that is a woman. Dry her up quickly! The wetness and water contents on her is cousing my antennas to detonate. Please hurry fused out Axis. Here Pour some sand and go get some leaves from those shrubs. Skinny commanded his men. Yellow and green. As the two cosmic workers were acting to find the leaves. Skinny was using his electric vibrations to revive the womans body and at the same time the wetness on the woman who was Sarah Cunningham who along with Bill Cunningham and Omar Bin Mohammad the three so called terrorist fugitives from the old earth world September 11, 2001 twin tower bombings was drying up. Sarah began to be revived but not till Axis was deja vuing his past earthly orgins. Axis remembers being in his mothers womb in a triangler dimentional deep ocean. The triangle was the "Axis of good". Is were he got his name from the cosmic powers. The triangle was called the "Bermuda Triangle". This was a place between Cuba and the state of Florida in the old American continent of the old earth world. Now! He remembered! The picture was comming in clear. The woman washed on the shore was his old earthly mother. Sarah Cunningham was his human mother. Axis recovered from his fusion and ran up quickly to the shore to meet his lost remembered past life mother and to reconnect with memories. This would be good also. For the cosmic powers. Although Axis and the intergalactic cosmic sapians did not feel pain or any emotion much less love or hate. They did charish memory. In fact the reason for Axis being here at the island station as they called it. That was the old earthly world. Was to gather data from the old earthtime.

Hi! Hi! Mother! Earthly mother! I am Axis! I am your son of the old concieved world. I beg your pardon. Huh? Where am I? Sarah reaching out her hand. Crawling out with her naked body from the sandy beach. Oh! My god I am naked. I have no clothe on. Don't worry earthly mother. We are cosmic sapians. We have no emotions or feelings. We are all magnetic. We don't see or feel sexuallity. Who are you. What are you talking about? My name is Sarah Cunningham. Where is my Father and my husband. Bill and Omar were unconcious for now. But were being treated by yellow and green the two crew cosmic sapians.

They are being revived woman Sarah. Skinny replyed. Revived? I don't remember were I came from. Am I in Hawaii? burped out Sarah.

No. Memory mother. You are in what used to be the old planet called earth. Where you are laying now. Used to be called America. A great catastrophy and a world war destroyed most of the world. This is all that is left of it. And some other Islands abroad. My name is Axis. And I and my crew are called the intergalactic cosmic sapians. We come here to this planet to take data for research purposes back to the cosmic dementional plain. "Axis explaining to Sarah."

I beg your pardon? Is this some sort Hollywood movie. Or what? Why you look so weird? Sarah replyed. Get me some clothe. I am freezing. My God! And why that is my daddy laying there. What are you doing to him weirdo? Sarah telling yellow the cosmic sapian. Leave my daddy alone. Bill was being revived as Omar with electrical vibrations. Power that came out off the cosmic sapians arms.

Memory mother! Fused out Axis. You don't know who I am. But my memory data tells me of a human woman named Sarah Cunnngham who had an affair with an Egyptian man Named Omar Bin mohammad. Omar the man was a religious person. And you my memory mother were a cosmetic business owner. I am getting this data from your electricity. What? Sarah blasted out. Yes memory mother. You both fell in with this emotion humans call love. And mated as humans do. You carried me around for a few days then you were in a fatal crash airplane accident in what we call the "Axis of good" dimention. And you called it "The Bermuda Triangle".

I was born in this triangle and went into the future life. which is where I am now. I really have no age or time. You my memory mother and your friends have but ten hours to live. Then you will evaporate back into the earths gases.

By this time Bill and Omar had awaken from there ocean spell. What is this you are saying sir? And who in the hell are you? Why do you look so weird? And why are we laying here naked on this beach? blasted Bill.

Sarah then tryed telling her father Bill Cunningham and Omar the whole story of how they got to this lonely deserted beach shore.

Then Bill remembered vaguely of the concorde flight and He Where is Henri and the rest of the crew cryed out Bill. We are fused. "Fused meaning the cosmic antennas having static." But there was only you and a couple of other men with you who died moments ago. Said Axis. Was one Henry lashed out Bill. Whats it matter we are all going to die in ten hours jumped up Sarah from the sandy beach shore. Lets have a look around before we go. What is that big white space ship over there? Asked Sarah. Looking at a space Craft parked inland by the greenery trees.

That is my space ship memory mother. Please come and join me. You must be hungry. All we have is what food there is around this island. And some fish from the sea. We cosmic sapians do not eat this planets food. All we consume is memory Data. Please come and join me.

Well ok my computer son. I have alot of memory shusi food for you. Ha, ha, ha. What have I gone nuts? Ten hours hey? Come on daddy and Omar. We would! Have to parish in the Bermuda Triangle. This life here must be the next step before we get hell! Ha? He, he, he.

The Island where the intergalactic cosmic forces were doing their data research. Was a cute place. Kind of like times of the dinasuar days. The days very young and sunny. Their was no seasons nor nights. Every day was the same. Very sunny and perfect temperture.

Here we are triggered." Axis". For you my memory mother I have the perfect table for you to sit on. Just call me mother. That is if I am your mother. A memory sounds kind of morbid. As you wish mother. Said Axis. And call Omar father and your grand daddy granpa! As you wish. We are here to serve.

Now we have some barries and fruits that grow in the wild. How about some fish milk? Humm I need to go potty first complained Sarah. Well I know what that is. Well don't go potty. So we have no rest rooms. So if you would like to go back into the greenery. Their is much privacy. fused out Axis. What privacy? look at your mother she is stark naked. Cryed out Sarah. Well let me go out there then.

Bill and Omar in the mean time were getting aquainted with the environment. 'This is quite a place spoke out Omar. Its like something out of a movie. The ancient Egyptians spoke of this kind of place in their books. Yea, well so did Plato the Greek philosopher and many others. I just want to go home. Say big fellow. Which way is it to Israel. I want to go home there.

I over heard you speaking granpa. Israel, Egypt, The lost continent of atlantas, America and many others are all comming but in a different form. When the new earth and world is greated for you. What are you saying my son Axis? Sarah returning from reliefing herself.

I am saying that in exactly eight hours. You my family will be reincarnated into immortal bodys. The bodys you now will be lost forever. But your souls and spirits will be reborn into the new world. In the new world there will be no war or pain. Religion and philosophy, ambition and power and greed will not exist. Government will be by just love. Well love is from god. Is there no god in the new world? Asked Omar. God is in all and for all. And its love will manifest in a peaceful world.

This is like a dream. I don't know if I am really in it. Now tell me Axis. Am I dead now? Is this hell? Proclaimed Sarah. No mother. This life that you were washed ashore in. Is an extention of the old earth life. You three family members and myself are the only ones that escaped the great world catastrophy. We are in the year 2050 and what they used to call A.D.

Oh! I see. Explained Bill. This is that funnie place where all those lost ships and people disappeared called the "Bermuda Triangle". But I don't see anyone of them around. Thats true. Fused out Axis. They all have become cosmic data. All those lost souls you heard about in the Bermuda Triangle are part of a cosmic program. That will bring new life to the new world of peace. And the first born in this new life will be you. And will we all lok like you? No offence Axis said Omar. What about our grandchild? Cryed Bill. Yes my baby that was in my womb? Said Sarah. And my son Omar breathed out.

Axis perceiving that his family did not understand his teaching and education. Yelled out! Your son! Is forever alive! You will know him and will dwell like you in the new world as a child like the rest of you in new immortal human bodys. In the new world there is no mating or sexual desires. Everyone is born out of cosmic order. There in the new world there is no death either. Every one does not get older nor ages. Everyone gets younger and lighter. Now come. We have but a few hours. I must take your data before we go into the new world cosmic order. Please lay here in my labratory table. I must take your contents.

Ok! let us have a conference Axis. Acknowleged Sarah. We really don't know you. And we will not go for some damn nightmare we might be in. We will huddle up and discuss this.

Ok be prompt. For in exactly six hours you will no longer be. Replied Axis.

In the huddled conference Bill and Omar were confused as to what was going on. Sarah was the only one who dared to take risk at this time and as always. For some reason Bill and Omar believed that they were in some dream and not really there.

There was arguing, fighting and sobbing. finally the reply came.

We are ready. Sarah being the spokes person. We have decided that I only should go into your so called new cosmic world. My daddy and my husband will stay in the old world and follow their nationality given god conscious. Ok fine mother. We must blast off. I need to make some arragements. Say goodbye to the family. Their souls will not be dated. They will go where their god given conscious directs them.

You and I mother will become one and enjoy eternity in the world of love.

Sarah and her intergalactic cosmic son Axis and his two helpers yellow and green boarded the flying space ship. And flew into the blue sky.

Omar Bin Mohammad and William "Bill" Cunningham along with skinny Axis manager stayed behind in the lost paradise of the Bermuda Triangle. Omar and Bill never really died ten hours after they were washed ashore. As Axis had warned. They lived there forever like eternity. Perhaps Sarah was right. "That", That lost Island. Americas remnant shores. was the next step to hell.

THE END

ABOUT THE AUTHOR

The author was born In Indio California U.S.A. And the book One tear for God, Trillion for America" Is science fiction short story terror romantic fantasy. Was written by "Gilbert Luna Alvarez" who at the time of writing the short story was 52 years young. In the summer of August 2002.

"Gil" as some call him has won a international recognition award for poetry. And has studied in Acting schools in Hollywood California.

Gil. Alvarez

Printed in the United States
By Bookmasters